Roy's Independence Day

a Night Stalkers holiday romance

by

M. L. Buchman

Copyright 2016 Matthew Lieber Buchman
Published by Buchman Bookworks, Inc.

All rights reserved.
This book, or parts thereof,
may not be reproduced in any form
without permission from the author.

Discover more by this author at:
www.mlbuchman.com

Cover images:
Paris Fireworks At Eiffel Tower © Dudau | Dreamstime.com
Helicopter over Baghdad © U.S. Army | Flickr
Sparkler © Denys Prokofyev | Dreamstime.com
Beautiful Couple In Each Other's Arms
© Teksomolika | Dreamstime.com

Buchman Bookworks

Other works by M. L. Buchman:

The Night Stalkers
The Night Is Mine
I Own the Dawn
Daniel's Christmas
Wait Until Dark
Frank's Independence Day
Peter's Christmas
Take Over at Midnight
Light Up the Night
Christmas at Steel Beach
Bring On the Dusk
Target of the Heart
Target Lock on Love
Christmas at Peleliu Cove
Zachary's Christmas
By Break of Day
Roy's Independence Day

Firehawks
Pure Heat
Wildfire at Dawn
Full Blaze
Wildfire at Larch Creek
Wildfire on the Skagit
Hot Point
Flash of Fire

Delta Force
Target Engaged
Heart Strike

Thrillers
Swap Out!
One Chef!
Two Chef!

Deities Anonymous
Cookbook from Hell: Reheated
Saviors 101

Angelo's Hearth
Where Dreams are Born
Where Dreams Reside
Maria's Christmas Table
Where Dreams Unfold
Where Dreams Are Written

Eagle Cove
Return to Eagle Cove
Recipe for Eagle Cove
Longing for Eagle Cove
Keepsake for Eagle Cove

SF/F Titles
Nara
Monk's Maze

Sign up for the newsletter to receive news and free items:
www.mlbuchman.com

Chapter 1

"Check out this. Southwest Gate."

By the tone over his radio headset, there was no question what Roy was being asked to check out. Not some depressed loon looking for "suicide by cop" achieved by jumping the fence. Nor some a-hole who thought he could actually cover the seventy yards between the fence and the White House without tripping a dozen alarms and alerting the ground teams.

Secret Service officer Roy Beaumont swung his sniper rifle around until he could see the Southwest Gate. He had the broadest field-of-view of the grounds from his perch on the roof of the Residence. Hank lay on the East Wing roof and wouldn't see squat, which would totally bum him out. Fernando's post on the West Wing roof had prime sightlines to the Southwest Gate. Mike was on the other side of the roof facing Pennsylvania Avenue and Lafayette Square and couldn't see this direction at all. Mike's was the most boring post because idiots always came across the wide South Lawn, rather than bolting for the short crossing to the North Portico, probably because of the attraction of the Oval Office overlooking the South Lawn.

As Secret Service counter snipers, they were set up for overlapping fields of surveillance and fire. They provided overwatch protection for the ground security teams, but their primary duty was to monitor the distant stretches of D.C. in search of threats. Any decent sniper could attack from a half mile away, a good one from a full mile or more. The shot could be taken from a hotel window or a parked van. It was the counter sniper's job to find them before they found the White House.

And on the incredibly long, boring watches, they also had overlapping views of any distraction. Sometimes it was a cute kid with a balloon out on The Ellipse (and it never hurt that cute kids often had cute moms in tow). Or a gaggle of dumb-ass protestors whining about something the Secret Service snipers couldn't even figure out from their signs—they really needed better PIOs, Public Information Officers. It could even be a cool car, though after a while it took a lot to be cool. By the fortieth or fiftieth Ferrari to swing past the White House even that sweet ride began to pale. Only one thing didn't.

Roy spotted her through his open left eye and let instinct guide the rifle scope to her face so that he could see her with his right eye. No question who Fernando was on about, just the way the woman walked was something special.

Monday morning on the last day of June had dawned beneath a brilliantly blue sky which left Washington D.C. sparkling. By midday it would be cooking his brains lying out on the roof on overwatch, but for the moment the day felt fresh and alive.

And the woman walking up from the Southwest security gate embodied life. There was a spring in her step. She wore professional clothes, which at the White House seemed to be synonymous with damned dull, but even they couldn't hide this woman. A shock of dark red hair, which gathered fire-gold highlights from the summer sunlight, framed her fair complexion. Her shape was very nice indeed and even professional clothes couldn't hide her overall fitness. He scanned down. Good legs wrapped in sheer hose, runner's or cycler's legs. Despite the youth of her face, hers wasn't the wild energy of some teen or twenty; this was a woman grown and powerful, and she absolutely knew it.

"Damn!"

"Told ya," Fernando sounded very pleased, as he should. This woman was prime material.

"Shit, man. Can't see a thing from here." Hank was definitely missing out.

Suddenly the woman was gone from the scope. She'd jinked sideways out of his view fast enough to mistrack even his sniper instincts.

Roy scanned the sidewalk, but he saw no cause such as someone else in her way or an unexpected mountain lion on the South Lawn. He re-centered on her face.

This time she was looking right at him with brown eyes beneath strong brows and she looked eight kinds of pissed. She gave him the finger, then disappeared out of sight into the West Executive Avenue entrance to the West Wing.

He laughed. Not one in a thousand noticed the snipers lying on the White House roof—though they were always there if the President or First Lady was in residence. If either of them came out, whether to walk the gardens or to cross to Marine One, a full SWAT team would be up here as well. No planned movement today, so it was just the snipers and the sky. The few people who picked out the counter snipers typically cowered down and scuttled a bit. Not this one.

Attitude. A hot redhead with attitude. A seriously fine start to a long summer watch.

"Enjoying something about the view, Agent Beaumont?"

Any warmth of the morning drained out of Roy as he rolled over to look up at the speaker. How six-two of barrel-chested, bad-ass senior agent moved so quietly was a constant mystery to all of the counter snipers. Dressed in a charcoal gray three-piece, the head of the Presidential Protection Detail looked completely out of place on the White House roof and yet there was no question that he absolutely ruled the roost.

"It's," Roy cleared his throat and tried again. "It's a beautiful day to be sitting overwatch, sir."

"Uh-huh."

The guy must be getting way too old if a hot woman didn't do it for him. Though Roy had seen his wife, Agent Beatrice Anne Belfour, and she was a seriously fine piece of agent.

"It's not nice to be pointing your weapon at civilians." Rumor was the President wouldn't even make the crossing to the Marine One helicopter if Frank Adams wasn't at his side. It would take a better man than Roy to argue with the leader of the PPD. Or maybe a dumber one—as he could feel himself about to do just that.

"How else are we supposed to assess civilians on the grounds without pointing our weapons at them?" He did his best to sound completely innocent. He had binoculars close to hand, but the Nightforce rifle scope on his heavily modified Remington 700—called a JAR by the Secret Service for "Just Another Rifle"—was much stronger and offered a superior view. And why in all creation was he teasing his boss? Maybe he really enjoyed getting in trouble as so many of his ex-girlfriends had told him. Crossing Frank Adams was a sure way to pull guard detail on a Congressional aide—a truly meaningless assignment.

Frank Adams' eyes scanned the distance over Roy's head as if reprimanding Roy from turning away from his post. How were you supposed to please a guy who wanted everything perfect all the time and wouldn't even respond to a bit of banter? Roy sighed and rolled back onto his stomach. The guy was a typical, senior-level square with no sense of humor… or hot women.

The silence was so long Roy almost turned to see if Adams still loomed behind him or had slipped away as silently as he'd appeared.

"Yep. I never solved that problem," Adams finally broke the morning stillness. "Beware pretty women; they can be hell on ya."

Roy did glance over his shoulder to see a bemused smile on Adams' face—the guys would never believe him because it was a known fact Frank Adams didn't smile. He decided silence was his best option and turned back to his sweep of the grounds.

"Met my wife at the wrong end of a gun, Roy," Adams sounded pretty damned pleased about it. "Just be careful of what you're looking at."

"Yes, sir." Hard to imagine someone pulling a weapon on Adams and expecting to live through it. Though Roy had met his wife—the head of the First Lady's Protection Detail—and maybe Adams had been the one lucky to survive.

It was only after Adams silently departed that Roy realized that the head of the PPD had actually used his first name. Roy hadn't known he even knew it.

# # #

Sienna Arnson made it from the White House entrance to the Oval Office without taking a single breath. Ten minutes in security, another fifteen to sign and countersign the receipt of her permanent badge, and seven more waiting in the outer office with the President's three secretaries for company. New breath-holding world record! And if she didn't remember how to breathe very soon…

"Maybe I'll be the first ever person to faint on the Oval Office rug."

"No. You wouldn't be the first," an amused voice said from close by her elbow.

She'd thought she was alone except for the secretaries diligently focused on whatever mayhem lay on their desks this morning.

"Good morning, Daniel," She'd met White House Chief of Staff Daniel Darlington III several times before, enough that she felt more at ease for his presence. She risked a small breath that did nothing to ease all of the tension of her first day serving in the White House. He was the sort of person who everyone called by his first name. Daniel did that to people, even angry senators demanding Presidential access and being told "no." At the moment she appreciated it. He was desperately handsome, surfer blond, intensely brilliant, and invariably kind.

"Who before me?"

"Well, me for one," he bowed as if fainting in front of the President would be an honor. "My first time in the Oval was the interview that jumped me from being the ex-assistant to the President's recently deceased first wife to being the new Chief of Staff. In fact, maybe I'm still locked away in a rubber room and dreaming all of this. Oh, I do like the sound of that. Is this Walter Reed Hospital by any chance?"

Sienna laughed with him, but knew the feeling. She'd worked her ass off to get here, but it still didn't seem real. To make it to—

"You can go in now," one of the secretaries waved her forward.

She took the first step, but Daniel didn't accompany her. "Aren't you coming?"

"In a minute. You go ahead," he waved her on.

"Bravery is taking action when you're scared spitless," she whispered to herself as there was no way she could spit right now even if her life depended on it. Just one of a hundred lessons her father had drilled into her over the years; drilled being the operative word. He'd been a Marine Corps captain by the time she was born. Now he was a brigadier general. Being a grownup in her mid-thirties hadn't slowed down his need to provide advice for every single occasion. The wonder was that this piece actually had relevance at the moment.

Squaring her shoulders—and ignoring Daniel's friendly chuckle as if he had read her mind—she proceeded through the door. And made it two steps before stumbling to a halt.

You've been here before! The internal shout did nothing to unglue her feet from where they'd become rooted on the glossy hardwood floor. Five years ago she had accompanied her father here when he became the commander of HMX-1—the group responsible for the Marine One fleet of helicopters. Kathleen Matthews had still been alive then. Oddly, the first First Lady of President Peter Matthews had left the Oval Office décor untouched. It had looked as plain as day on Sienna's first visit.

The President's second wife had clearly taken a hand. The bulk of the Oval Office lay to her right. The two couches and circle of armchairs that had been in blah-beige were now a rich, chocolate-brown leather. Their sharp contrast to the light walls and bright parquet floor felt much more powerful, as if to say "serious work is done here." The prior administration's selection of soothing pastel paintings had once again been replaced by the portraits of George, Abe, and J.F.K. who all looked down at her from their perches high on the wall as if to ascertain she wasn't about to royally screw up.

First day on the job, boys. No promises.

There was no fire in the grand fireplace, but the broad mantel had two stunning bouquets of peonies that somehow only emphasized that this was the seat of Presidential power.

Geneviève Beauchamp Matthew's hand had clearly been at work here. Sienna wanted to grow up to be just like the First Lady. But as she was neither a tall, curvaceous French-Vietnamese nor a senior level director of UNESCO World Heritage Centre, that wasn't going to happen.

The view to her left was even more daunting. Backed by the morning sunlight sweeping in through the curved windows, President Peter Matthews was standing by his desk, leaning down to make some quick notes. It was alarming how much he'd aged. Elected as one of the youngest Presidents in history, barely past the legal age of thirty-five. The seven long years since had definitely taken their toll, but there was still an intensity and a liveliness to him. With just six more months until the elections, he'd be retired in eight. When he was, she'd be out of a job, but she didn't care.

Sienna felt a gentle shove against her back and stumbled forward as Daniel gave her a push. She turned to tell him to cut it out and she had just a moment to see his smile before he closed the door on her heels. She wished she'd thought to flip him the finger before it closed, just as she had to that sniper on the White House roof. Her father had taught her situational awareness, making the sniper easy to spot. But when he had aimed his weapon at her, it had been completely infuriating. Who did the swine think she was?

It was also her first day on the job and being treated as a threat had just pissed her off all the more. When he'd quickly recentered his aim on her, she somehow knew he wasn't looking at her as a threat but rather as something to leer at. It had tipped her over the edge. If he thought for a second that—

"Hello, Sienna," the President tossed his pen down as if the Roosevelt Desk was just…his desk.

"Hello, Mr. President." She'd get a handle on this in a minute.

"I don't suppose you'd be willing to call me by my given name?" He made it sound sad and plaintive. "My wife will barely use it because I was already President when we met. Please?" He tried a pout which didn't work at all on his strong face.

"Not a chance, Mr. President." Maybe she'd never get a handle on this.

"I was afraid of that. Well, I do apologize for bringing you in so late in the administration, but your predecessor as my National Security Advisor seemed to think a shot at being the next senator from North Carolina was more important. Can't imagine why."

It was something of a surprise that the home of the nation's largest fort, Fort Bragg, actually liked the former NSA. While the National Security Advisor wasn't actually a part of any intelligence agency—rather an appointee of the President—the military still generally despised NSAs on principal. The fact that he had been a retired two-star Army general before becoming the NSA probably hadn't hurt, but it would also put her at a distinct disadvantage having no direct military service herself.

The President was clearly awaiting some sort of a response. It was definitely her turn to speak.

"It will be…is an honor, sir."

"I'm just very glad to have you aboard. I really do appreciate the skillset you bring and not just as an interim fill-in. I can't afford anything less than the best in your position."

"Thank you, Mr. President." Sienna felt about six feet tall with the compliment, but her nerves downgraded that to her normal five-six within seconds. Then they once again threatened to make her feel seven years old and four feet tall.

"The nerves go away eventually," he remarked with disarming empathy. "Just ask this man," the door opened behind her.

Daniel, at last. Thank the lor—

"He's lying," Vice President Zachary Taylor said as he walked into the Oval. "I didn't hear a word, but I wouldn't trust him if I were you." His flat Coloradan accent gave no hint as to whether he was joking.

"Why not?" Sienna was feeling too disoriented to make sense of anything at the moment.

"Eight years ago he chose me as a running mate. It puts me in a prime seat for this election. Care to tell me how that makes the least little bit of sense? You tell me how and I'll take it back."

"I can't imagine how it would, Mr. Vice President." Which the moment she said it, she knew it had come out all wrong. "I meant—"

"No. No." The Vice President laughed aloud and held out his hands to stop her. "That was perfect, don't mess it up by trying to straighten it out." He dropped into one of the two armchairs at the head of the room, the other clearly for the President by its somewhat more dominant position.

Sienna studied the two men. Both were tall, dark-haired, and dressed in immaculate suits, but you would never mix them up.

All of the President's Washington, D.C. upbringing showed in a formality that defined him despite his attempt to put her at ease.

Zachary Taylor looked as if he was ready to slouch his way onto a horse, though she knew he'd barely ridden prior to meeting Daniel's sister just last winter. They had been married in May at a small ceremony on her family's farm. The fact that the Darlingtons were one of the first families of Tennessee and the Vice President was rapidly becoming the presumptive nominee of his party, had of course made the event headline news around the world.

There had been a great deal of scuttlebutt about the wedding being motivated by the upcoming election, but her father had put the kibosh on that. "Never seen a pair like the two of them. They both get so mushy together a man has to look the other way. The President's no less in love with his wife, but they are two very driven, very serious people. The Vice President and Anne Darlington-Taylor are…" he searched for a word he was comfortable with, "…gentler. No less impressive, just gentler."

Sure enough, while waiting for the meeting to begin, the two men were talking about their wives.

"Anne and the First Lady are plotting something for the Fourth, but they aren't letting me in on it. How about you, Peter?" So, the Vice President was on a first name basis with the President. Braver man than she was.

"Not a word, Zack. Of course with our luck, it will all be for the World Heritage Centre and not a thing for us. Maybe we need a plan of our own."

"I'll bring the beer if you bring the dogs…but I'll wager they'll surprise the hell out of us just like always."

The two men shared a smile of happy complacency, so sure of their spouses.

The President and the Vice President had an almost Laurel and Hardy smoothness to them as they continued bantering with the other people arriving for the meeting. The two men had grown very close ever since the Italian avalanche that had rocketed the already popular Vice President into the stratosphere for his rescue efforts. Again, something had changed behind the scenes that she'd only been able to observe externally.

Well, now she was a step closer to the inside for all the good it did her.

And her father had been right, the Vice President was completely mushy about his wife. Why couldn't she ever attract mushy? She attracted either the ones so driven that their career meant far more to them than she did. Of course, she was the same way, so the driven types made for a bad combination both ways. The other kind she fell for were the total dogs, like that damned sniper. Worse, she fell for them every time. Well, not this one, mostly because she wouldn't have time.

She was now the new National Security Advisor to the President of these United States of America and by god she was going to be the best one ever, even if it only lasted seven months. Six months and twenty-one days. A lot could happen in so much time.

With only a slight hint from Daniel—once he finally arrived—she took the position on the couch closest to the President's chair as the others settled in their familiar places. Secretaries of State, Defense, and Homeland Security. Treasury, economics advisor, and the Directors of National Intelligence and Drug Policy. Even the White House Chief of Counsel and the U.N. Ambassador were in attendance. Last in was General Brett Rogers, the Chairman of the Joint Chiefs of Staff, arriving precisely one minute early. His preferred place was standing between the Vice President and Daniel. Everyone had come to the first meeting with the new NSA. The entire National Security Council was in attendance, the statutory attendees and the regulars, as well as the advisors and the additional participants who were typically present only when needed.

But no pressure.

It was probably too late now to get out of the meeting by fainting.

There would be no nice smooth handoff from the former advisor to her. He was spending the start of his new senatorial campaign at home with a late spring flu. She was on her own.

Greetings of different qualities vibrated through the air and she did her best to calibrate and quantify them. Director of Homeland Security and National Intelligence were old college frat buddies who could barely stand each other. General Brett Rogers didn't smile at anyone and kept strictly to himself. She knew from prior meetings with him over the years at her father's house that he was taciturn by nature, not temperament. He would speak when he had something to say but not a moment before or after.

For the thousandth time Sienna wondered at the tack she herself should take. There were many here ready to discount her. She was the youngest NSA of the four female NSAs there had ever been and the only woman in the room this morning. She also knew from a lifetime of experience that the only female types discounted more thoroughly than blondes were redheads. She'd considered dying her hair to brown, but for better or worse had stuck with natural, dark red, and it was too late to change it now.

She would be…

She glanced at the gorgeous grandfather clock that stood guard by the door closest to the President's desk and would have overwhelmed any lesser room than the Oval Office. It was straight up eight a.m., the scheduled start of the meeting.

She would be…herself, just as her father always described her: a natural-born hard-ass.

"Good morning, gentleman. Mr. Vice President and Mr. President." She raised her voice to cut through the conversations. The room quieted as she flipped open the cover on her tablet computer and tapped it awake.

General Rogers gave her a terse nod of approval for the timely start—an unexpected show of support.

"Item One on today's agenda: the South China Sea and what the Chinese are doing there *this* time." A hard-ass with a sense of humor. That worked for her.

Daniel snorted with a suppressed laugh.

That was a better start than she'd expected. Then she started in on the reports she'd spent most of last night and this morning assembling into a coherent presentation.

It only took a few minutes before she and the rest of the group were fully engaged by the information she had assembled. Input and suggestions sounded in rapid-fire succession and she fielded each one, able to answer most and flagging the strays for further research. Thoughts of anything else faded away: May morning, Oval Office, new job, and jerk Secret Service snipers.

Sienna had many lovers who had accused her of "being the job." It had never been more true than her first moments as the National Security Advisor sitting in the Oval Office.

And she was fine with that.

# # #

Ninety minutes on. Ninety minutes off.

Roy's sniper detail rotated down into the Secret Service room in the basement of the West Wing every hour and a half. Not that time off was actually "off." Lunch hour was the only true break they ever came close to having, and even that rarely happened.

There was always paperwork, studying new threats, or helping the prep team for the next Presidential outing. It would be so much easier if the country's leaders just locked themselves in on Inauguration Day and didn't come out until their replacement trundled their belongings in the door four or eight years later. It didn't work that way so the preparation tasks were endless.

By his final watch on the roof that day, he was sure he'd missed her—best looking woman he'd seen in a long while. A bummer, but that was the job. Wouldn't have minded another look no matter what Frank Adams thought about it.

The city was emptying. Rush hour madness had set in.

Roy didn't exactly relax his vigilance, but for some reason, crazies tended to stage their attacks early in the day. Maybe by the time they had their cappuccino or overdose of McGrease, the little aliens in their heads would leave off with their "special" instructions for a while. Now it was just the steady drone of distant traffic. The White House and the wide grounds made it a relatively quiet haven among the commuter madness.

This bubble of silence always made him think of hunting back home in Hardwick, Vermont. He and his father had spent endless hours tracking through the forests around the backside of Lake Elligo. Sometimes with rifles, sometimes bow and arrow, but most often simply armed with fishing poles. His father rarely spoke, except to instruct, and Roy had come to love the peace of those times.

Lying here atop the White House roof, much of his view was of the big white oaks on the White House lawn. A manicured reminder of the oak, maple, and Norway pine forests of home. As evening settled over the city, he tried to imagine himself setting up camp under a lean-to alongside a fast rushing stream thick with dinner still swimming in the cool water.

Fernando's double click over the microphone had his attention swinging before he even wholly returned to D.C. A little more circumspect, he kept his rifle close to hand and slipped out his binoculars.

Again, there was no mistaking her. She'd been inside the bubble of the White House for a full day, which he knew to be exhausting, but she was still going a mile a second.

Halfway to the gate, she glanced back over her shoulder and slammed to a halt as if she'd hit a glass wall.

For a long moment, she was looking at the White House itself, her grin as wide as a little girl's given a brand new toy. Then her eyes tracked upward.

Her smile shifted. No less radiant, but now she looked… dangerous.

She very deliberately scratched at the side of her nose with her extended middle finger, then whirled on her heel and was gone.

He could hear Fernando's laugh on the murmuring D.C. air though he was stationed over a hundred feet away.

# # #

Sienna lay on her Georgetown bed, her body vibrating with exhaustion. The National Security Council meeting had been scheduled at a full hour, and she closed it at exactly fifty-nine minutes. It was an act that seemed to take everyone by surprise, except for Daniel who nodded in thanks—clearly very protective of his boss' schedule.

The President had welcomed her once more and they'd all filed out as his next meeting filed in. General Rogers fell in beside her as they moved through the outer office.

"If you have a moment?"

She'd hoped to try and find her office. She had met with the former NSA a number of times there. It was also where Daniel, the President, and others had interviewed her, but now it was finally hers and she wanted to see it. Instead, she followed the general.

That "moment" had led to two hours in the Situation Room. She'd been too busy trying to keep up with his sharp mind to be shocked by the plainness of the room. So many movies and television shows portrayed the darkly mysterious room with hand scanners, mahogany tables, leather armchairs, and massive screens covered in situational analyses. Beyond the pair of Marine guards standing at attention outside the door, it was about as undramatic as could be.

In truth, it looked like any standard white conference room with a few too many phones and a few too many television screens against one wall.

The general, who must have had a detailed awareness of her resume, had proceeded to grill her as if for a job interview. Dartmouth, Yale, Oxford. Rand Corp think tank. Some time in Stratfor studying geopolitical influences to forecast military hotspots. Through her father's connections and her own, she'd arranged for a three-year study on normalizing the six US Commands. She'd spent six months each at: USNORTHCOM and USSOUTHCOM which covered North and South America, USAFRICOM, USEUCOM which included all of Russia, USCENTCOM which was the hell of southwest Asia, and USPACOM from the West Coast to Japan, China, and Australia with Antarctica tossed in for good measure.

At some point she couldn't identify, her interview with the Chairman of the Joint Chiefs of Staff had shifted from interrogation to consultation. Having proven her understanding of the big picture to General Roger's satisfaction, he was soon testing his own understanding of power centers and friction motives against her own observations.

Unlike any other conference room anywhere, each time the general called out to the apparently empty room, "We need to see a map of the distribution of Chinese forces from Hong Kong to Australia," or "What is the current estimated stability of the ruling regime in the Congo?" hidden Marine Corps intelligence officers would leap into action. Within moments the information would be on the main screen. At her own request, a key tabulation of activities of NATO versus EU alliances was pushed down from the big screen onto her tablet computer. She could get used to this.

When the general departed with no more than a solemn nod of approval, she suspected she'd passed a test more stringent than Daniel's and the President's original interviews.

She'd spent a quiet hour in the Situation Room—in the Situation Room!—working on better answers to some of the general's unresolved questions. Or at least unearthing better questions of her own.

Her next foray to reach her office passed close by the Vice President's. His assistant, the rather daunting Cornelia Day, had flagged her down and asked if she had plans for lunch.

She didn't have plans to eat…ever, especially not with the way her head was already whirling. She'd only met the Vice President a few times and had never sat with him one-on-one. Cornelia took advantage of Sienna's brief hesitation to conduct her into Zachary Taylor's White House office, decorated in what she finally decided might best be called, early tongue-in-cheek style.

The very first thing she noticed was an HO-gauge trainset on a lovely 1700s table of Quaker simplicity and craftsmanship. It resided in a place of honor close by the big window facing the Eisenhower Executive Office Building and she suspected that if she asked about it, they might never find another topic. So she glanced at the rest of the office.

There were stunning photos of the Colorado Rockies and also the softer hills that she could only assume were near his wife's family residence in Tennessee. There were photos of skiers and the two of them on horseback. If she'd seen a full set of horse tack or a pair of downhill skis tucked behind the door—she checked and there weren't—she wouldn't have been surprised. There was one picture of the former Captain Zachary Taylor, looking very official and handsome in his dress whites with an alarming number of service ribbons. It had cropped up in the news a lot after the Italian disaster. But it was another photo, hung close beside the trainset, that caught her attention and finally gave her the ability to speak.

"Why haven't I ever seen this one?" Not the most gracious of openings. To cover her gaffe, Sienna pointed to the image of a very handsome and somewhat younger Zachary Taylor with three other men all clowning around. They wore flight suits and were clearly enjoying each others' company too much to pose seriously in front of the massive Air Force rescue helicopter that must be theirs.

"Always struck me as a bit disrespectful. Our job was hauling out a lot of very hurt people. But my Anne"—again with the mushy tone—"insisted I put that one up."

Obviously she'd done all of the decorating, but Sienna wasn't going to tease the Vice President about that. "No. It makes what you did more human. You should definitely release it."

"Well, that makes two votes to my one. The President always said not to argue with women who we don't have two shakes of a rattler's tail chance of understanding anyway. I'll give it to my people." And Sienna learned that the Vice President gave full respect to his President when outside of Peter Matthews' presence.

His smile was easy to return. They spent most of lunch discussing favorite D.C. restaurants. In his own way, that too was an interview only a little less demanding than General Rogers'. In the hour she gained a real sense of the man and learned that he probably deserved all of the respect he received in the press.

Daniel had snagged her as she once more entered the hallway a mere twenty feet from her own office. He led her back to his office, thanked her for keeping the meeting on time (apparently the first National Security Advisor to do so in this administration—and perhaps any other), then introduced her to…she'd have to check her notes.

All afternoon she'd felt as if she'd been targeted by that sniper. This advisor…Wham! That superintendent…Bang! The Secretary of Defense (who clearly felt her age, gender, and having a pulse completely disqualified her for the job, though having a chest at least gave him something to look at)…Kaboom!

There were only three large offices on the west side of the West Wing's first floor: White House Chief of Staff, Vice President, and her own. She didn't make it there until six o'clock in the evening.

And yet as she'd walked out of the White House, with little more brain activity than one of her brother's zombie movies, she couldn't help but look back and smile.

Day One as the National Security Advisor.

Check!

And if she could avoid screwing up, there were still two-hundred and three more days to go until the next President's inauguration.

That's when she'd remembered the sniper and glanced up. Was it the same one? She had no idea as he was little more than a silhouette far above. At least there was no sniper rifle aimed at her this time, but his binoculars weren't exactly cruising back and forth across the lawn seeking trespassers. Flipping him off this morning in full view of the White House had been perhaps a little rash. So, she was more subtle about it this time.

She'd heard a second counter sniper on the West Wing's roof laugh, but for some reason it was the one stationed on the Residence who had caught her attention. She supposed it proved that the girl still had it if she kept him riveted so.

It had put a bounce in her step, which was all that sustained her until she had made it home.

She shouldn't have laid down in her suit; it would be too wrinkled to wear to the White House again without a trip to the dry cleaners if she lay here much longer. However, the thought of moving was even worse. Maybe if she just lay very still then it wouldn't crease. Not a problem; she wasn't sure if she'd ever move again.

She didn't have time to worry about suit wrinkles in the morning as she awoke with barely time to change out of her crumpled clothes before rushing out to the CIA for a round robin of briefings and meetings there. Next time she'd set an alarm *before* she lay down.

Chapter 2

R*oy kept an eye* out for the babe all week. No joy. The sniper's call of no clear sighting didn't begin to describe his pain.

Frank Adams had decided that riding Roy Beaumont's ass was his new duty assignment. Pretending to hate it was one of the requirements of such an assignment, but Roy was actually fascinated by the challenges.

Route planning was supposed to be a sniper's version of peeling potatoes or scrubbing toilets. It took a lot of time and infinite attention to detail. When moving the President around, he could never be moved by a predictable route. That meant before each trip, multiple routes had to be scouted. Then decisions were made about where to station blockades, agents, police, dogs, and overwatch counter snipers. The final decisions on that last point were made by CS technicians like himself, mostly staring at maps, photos, and 3D mapping software that would make an online map user wet their pants. He was suddenly Adams' sniper whipping boy for route reviews. Adams even flogged him through "lessons learned" reviews of previous route selections and how they could have been improved.

There was only one major drawback to the change in duties. Sometimes on break Fernando or even, god help him, Hank would tell him about sightings of Roy's "girlfriend."

His big mistake was denying any such thing.

Ever since, the guys rubbed it in every chance they had. All locker room shit. "He *lo-oves* her, but he don't even know her name!" "He so hot for her that he's humping his rifle at night." And on. And on. With no more imagination than a tree squirrel trying to hide a winter's worth of acorns from another tree squirrel.

It *was* aggravating to know she was one of the seventeen hundred people who worked at the White House and all he could do was sit in the Secret Service's basement office and wonder where. Not a chef, they would enter through the Main Residence. Nor one of the First Lady's staff, as they'd head for the East Wing. She was West Wing which narrowed it down to a thousand and change. Not in the Secret Service office—because otherwise he'd have seen her while poring over route maps until his eyes were redder than a winterberry—down to an even thousand.

If he was so poor at narrowing target selection as a sniper, he'd never have been allowed in the service at all, but he couldn't find a way to focus it down any more. So he fell back on his father's training as a hunter—sit still and wait. By the end of the week, he had run that option dry as well.

Fernando was right, he really needed to get a life. But even if Roy did, he should never have listened to his friend.

"Come on, man. You got to meet my cousin. She will love you." Uh-huh. Uh-huh. Fernando was one of those crazy Latino guys for whom every woman was somehow his "cousin."

"It's the Fourth, man." Anyone who could, pulled duty on the White House roof for the Fourth of July. From there, snipers had prime seats for the nation's Number One fireworks show above the Reflecting Pool and the Washington Monument.

"So? We gotta go out and make some fireworks. You wanta watch or do you wanta do?" Fernando's tone left no question about his choice.

Having too little common sense left by Friday night, he agreed to meet "Fernando's cousin." After the last watch, he showered and changed. Fernando just shook his head sadly. "You don't know how to dress up for the ladies, man. This girl, she is hot."

Jeans and black tennies along with a flannel shirt against the cool evening seemed fine to him, but apparently it was too country hick for Fernando who'd grown up in Philly. So Roy dug around in his locker and fished out a moderately fresh t-shirt that said USSS in bold letters across the back: United States Secret Service.

"Shit man. Kind of place we going, they see that, they all going to leave!"

Roy had worked damn hard to earn the right to wear that shirt, but could take Fernando's point. The last clean shirt he had said, "Snipers do it with precision."

"Now we're talking man," which told Roy exactly what sort of night it was going to be.

So he shrugged on his USSS jacket just for spite and Fernando groaned, but gave up protesting.

They hit a couple bars and knocked back a couple beers. As they worked their way down the food chain from bistro to bar to dive, he was pleased to see that his jacket did indeed clear out some of the chaff. More than once it opened up space at a crowded bar and Fernando admitted he might be onto something.

"How far down we going?" A back alley would be a step up from their present locale.

"Just warming you up, man. Don't any of you Vermont boys know how to party?"

Sure he did. You sat back somewhere quiet, which was most of Vermont, and you watched the stars with a six of beer and a friend to share it with. Or during the ski season you headed into the bars of Stowe and hit on snow bunnies there to ski the mountain and slide into a quick fling.

Fernando led him into a dance bar named Jake's Hole nowhere near the nice end of town, and D.C. had a whole lot of not nice. "Hole" was a compliment the place didn't deserve; it rated about a four for habitability, on a scale of a hundred. He, Fernando, and Hank grabbed a chunk of the bar to observe the local talent.

"I didn't believe you, hombre," he slapped Fernando on the back feeling all the camaraderie that happened after three beers. "The women here are all two Budweisers and above."

"Say what?"

"Old joke. How many Budweiser Clydesdales would it take to haul me away from the woman? They're tough horses; two is a pretty high number."

Fernando's smile was brilliant on his dark face, "I told you so, man. These are my cousins."

Some were indeed Latino, but others were Chinese slender or African dark. There were women who were more curve than woman, their bodies teasing with all there was to explore. There were long and lean ones who it was easy to imagine would wrap around your body where they'd cling until a man had nothing left to give. About the only type missing was an average white women. And there was absolutely no sign of a spirited, perfectly proportioned redhead.

He danced some, drank more, and wondered if the redhead was a better dancer than he was. He hoped so for her sake. Around beer six, the three-beer buzz was wearing thin and he decided that maybe the women here weren't as hot as he'd first thought. Or maybe they decided he wasn't. A couple took a run at him but didn't seem very committed to the effort. Or maybe he was the one who wasn't—couldn't tell and didn't care. They drifted away quickly. He ended up in a corner booth with Hank trading war stories and drinking depth bombs: a beer with a shot of whiskey dropped into the glass. Chug it down to get your shot back.

Fernando disappeared with some long-legged Latina about the time Hank lost all ability to form coherent words. Roy poured Hank into a taxi, prepaid the driver, and walked home in order to clear his head.

In less than four hours they'd completely trashed what might have been a lazy Friday night hanging out with the other snipers on rooftop watch and viewing the fireworks. The sun was gone and he heard the first boom of The National Mall's fireworks show when he was still several miles out. The only part of it he could see from here was the occasional red or blue glow on the horizon. Every once in a while there was a lull in the traffic and he could hear the distant rumble of an explosion. Around here he was just glad it wasn't gunfire.

He thought of tonight's White House counter sniper team with some envy. Even more envy for those who'd set up picnics in the town park of Hardwick. His hometown's fireworks shows were only everyone's reservation-bought roman candles and crackers, but it always made for a good picnic excuse by the lake as the fireworks sparkled over the water with sharp snaps and pops. He'd kissed his share of willing girls by the light of those homegrown firework shows.

Fernando was right about one thing: it was time for Roy to let go of his White House redhead fantasy.

Crap!

"Happy Independence Day, Roy," he told the dark city before beginning the long walk home.

Five long miles and the only thing that was clear by the end of it was that he was in for a doozy of a hangover in the morning.

It was the one thing he got right.

# # #

Sienna spent the Fourth buried in her office. With most of the staff on holiday, she closed her door against the other senior staff who—like her—didn't have a life and worked.

The heavy boom of the first firework and the sudden glare of light through her windows brought her back to reality. Stepping out into the hallway she was rapidly swept up in the tide headed out to the South Lawn. Many who'd had the day off had used their clearance to the grounds to bring their families to one of the prime viewpoints for the show. A large and merry crowd had gathered on the lawn.

The stars only barely showed above the city, but the South Lawn fountain backed by the Washington Monument and the distant Thomas Jefferson Memorial was one of the best night views in a city that truly shone at night.

Sienna had wound up near the First Family who had come out for the display. She sipped a beer that the Vice President gave her, judiciously for she'd barely eaten all day, and was thrilled when Daniel's wife stuffed a paper plate into her hand with a grilled burger and chips despite the late hour. There wasn't a bit of fancy, it was pure picnic comfort food—definitely the First and Second Ladies' doing—and a quick glance showed that they absolutely knew their men who were standing side by side enjoying their own burgers and brews. As the fireworks lit the sky with explosions like flowers, rings, and glowing horsetails, her thoughts had inevitably tracked to the roof.

She moved farther down the lawn to give the First Families some space…or so she told herself. It was only when she caught herself watching not the fireworks, but rather the briefly illuminated snipers on the roof, that she knew she was doing one of her fixation things. Somehow he'd become a symbol to her.

The world will be watching you, Sienna.
Thanks, Dad. Just the confidence builder I needed.

And that stupid sniper only served to reinforce her father's comments. It wasn't as if most people knew what a National Security Advisor was or did—hell, she hadn't until she'd been dropped into the role. After her first full week, she had to admit she still wasn't sure, but the Powers That Be had seemed pleased.

"Never argue with the Powers That Be," she told the distant sniper.

Earlier today Sienna's mom replied to her "Week One down. Doing fine!" text with a "You go, hon!" and a triple smiley emoticon that let Sienna feel every bit of her mom's joy. But Sienna knew that wouldn't hold Dad. General Edward Arnson was a man who liked to assess the status of any situation personally. She really didn't have time for it, but she caved after only a token resistance, knowing that she'd earned her Arnson persistence straight down the paternal line and there was no escaping the inevitable.

They'd agreed on a time to meet Saturday morning.

Mom was wise enough to leave the two of them to it.

Saturday morning they hit one of their regular spots, the Smithsonian National Air and Space Museum on the Mall. It was close by the Capitol Building—which always made her father grumble about "a waste of space." The museum was nearing the end of the renovation of the Boeing Milestones of Flight hall, but it was still roped off. So instead of meeting beneath the Apollo 11 Command Module, they met at the rope line in the hallway and looked in. The additions of the LEM lunar lander and the original Starship *Enterprise* shooting model made them both smile for different reasons.

"Most incredible thing I ever did as a young Marine," her father said gruffly. "I flew the secondary helo for two different Apollo recoveries, including that one right there," as if she didn't know he'd flown for that splashdown. Why else did they always meet here? "Got to watch the whole show from two hundred feet. Would have liked to have shaken their hands, but it was back when we still tucked them straight into isolation trailers for fear of them bringing back some space disease. Of course they had to get their camera moment crossing from the helo to the trailer, so it was a darned useless to-do but it played well on the media. Don't ever let the media control your decisions, Sienna. You hear me?"

"Sure, Pop. I know that."

As to her reason for smiling—her own crush on Jean Luc Picard—she kept to herself. Especially as this *Enterprise* was the wrong model—the NCC-1701 classic versus *The Next Generation's* NCC-1701-D.

While they stood and watched at the rope line, a pair of the exhibit handlers were lining up the *Enterprise* in an x-ray machine, imaging its interior structure section by section. They looked silly in their heavy lead aprons using machinery so archaic that it would never have been allowed on the show. She kept waiting for one of the technicians to just whip out a tricorder and get it done with.

She talked through with her dad what she felt she was free to discuss as they wandered out of the hall and into the "America by Air" exhibit. The early passenger liners, and nose cones for the 747 and some Airbus, weren't really of much interest to either of them. The second floor with its rovers and the more recent "Military Unmanned Vehicles" exhibit were more their speed. She really needed to get back to the White House to catch up. Or at least try. Her first week had buried her and even working the holiday had barely dented the backlog.

As they walked and talked, she found it odd to have the shoe on the other foot. She'd always been able to tell when her father had reached the limit of what he was allowed to tell her. It was just an understood part of being a general's daughter.

But now she was the one having to be careful about what she said. It wasn't a question of clearance, her father's went as high as hers, it was a matter of compartmentalization—which had its own logistical problems in running a command that she wasn't going to think about right now. So she told him more about the people than what they said, which was a mistake of a different color.

"Damn the man," her father growled. "Doesn't Hayward have any respect? I'll—"

"Do absolutely nothing, Pop!" Sienna stopped him in front of a bank of flight simulator rides with lines of children jostling for a chance to be next. "I know how to handle dirty old men, even when they are the misogynistic Secretary of Defense. I've run into enough of them over the years. If he hates me now, he'd really hate me after one of your 'talks.'"

"Could be. Could be," her father admitted, though he sounded grumpy about it. "What about that young whipper-snapper over there?"

Sienna could feel the tease, her father was always pointing out likely men—especially when it served to change the subject from somewhere uncomfortable such as his daughter no longer being twelve. It wasn't that he wanted her to be someone's wife—she'd confronted him on that. "Just want you to be as happy as your ma and I are, that's all."

She'd had a heart to heart with Mom as a backcheck. "Love the man to death, but don't marry a military man lest you have a penchant for being alone. But your father is a sweet man behind all his busyness being a general."

Sienna turned to follow her father's line of sight.

He *had* picked out a likely one. Sandy blond hair and six feet of solid, he was strong in a rough-hewn way. Which described his face as well. He would never be called handsome, if it wasn't for the smile he was aiming at the eight year old girl he was lifting off one of the simpler simulator rides—lifting her like she was made of helium not human despite her stoutness. He wore a badge, so he was helper, not parent.

His smile, Sienna decided, was lethal. As if to prove Sienna's observation, the young girl was completely smitten and did her level best to engage the man even as he helped an eager young boy aboard. He must be a docent—one of the thousand volunteers who helped keep the museums of the nation's capital running. As soon as the boy was settled, he didn't brush off the little girl, but instead knelt until they were eye level. It was awfully sweet.

Once the girl was gone off with her mother (with several backward glances, and not just from the little girl), he rose to his feet, though it looked like it cost him. A hard wince and a moment weaving with tightly closed eyes.

"Think he had a rough night last night," her father whispered, which with him meant that only the closest dozen or so people could hear him. Thankfully, this was D.C. and no one cared.

There was no question that he was hungover…but still taking time to be kind to the little girl. She liked that.

The docent checked on the boy then scanned the busy hall. His eyes didn't skim; they tracked steadily about the room, assessing everyone. She'd seen it often enough in her consultations with the US Commands to know that meant soldier or some other form of military training. Even police didn't move that way, or look so good doing it. Military yet still volunteering in another way—more points in his favor.

Her mother's admonition about military men slipped into her thoughts and slid away just as quickly. Advice was everywhere, decent guys were few and far between, especially ones who looked the way he did. He was definitely the sort of man who should always wear tight black t-shirts.

When his inspection reached her and her father, his gaze didn't slide by. Instead his blue eyes focused on her with a positive target lock. His eyes popped wide and his jaw dropped. Just like in a cartoon.

It forced a laugh out of her.

"You definitely have his attention," Pop grumbled in her ear.

She had. It happened to her on occasion, but never quite so dramatically. He took a half step in her direction, stopped, turned back to the boy he was obviously supposed to be watching, then back to her. Trapped.

"Are you going to put the poor man out of his misery?" Leave it to her father to take pity on a fellow soldier. Except her father wasn't a soldier, he was a Marine—a distinction she'd had clear in her head before she hit pre-school.

"I don't know, Pop. What has he done to deserve it? Hungover means he was drunk last night while I was working. Not the best recommendation." She made her decision and turned for the stairs up to the second story. As she moved past her dad, she whispered to him, "Is he dying yet?"

"Near to a coronary," he chuckled and moved up beside her.

She continued leading her father away.

"Have you got a good reason why we're moving so slow?"

"I'm not moving slow. I'm just taking my time to admire the exhibits."

"That's my gal," her father sounded quite pleased. "Hard-ass to the core." It was one of her father's highest compliments. She used to wonder how different her life might be if she wasn't; if she hadn't spent her entire childhood trying to live up to his "hard-ass" standard. It didn't mean she was nasty. It meant she demanded the absolute best of herself and everyone around her. And some hungover docent, no matter how nice he was to a little girl, wasn't going to come close.

She was just about to pick up the pace, when a hand touched lightly upon her arm.

"Excuse me, ma'am."

At the instant of contact she knew who it was.

Even that simple gesture riveted her attention on him. And it was a very nice view, other than his bloodshot eyes. His shoulders weren't particularly broad, but they were very strong. And the plain black t-shirt followed the taper of his waist down. His eyes, blue with distance, were a powerful statement in a strong face up close. Again she was struck by the strength of his rugged face, but she wasn't about to give ground just because he was so good-looking. Not handsome exactly, just extremely…male.

"Aren't you supposed to be watching the little children?"

"The museum is used to me being unreliable." He said it as if he was bragging.

"Oh, like that's a good thi—"

Her father nodded back toward the simulators. Another docent was there helping the children. She wasn't letting him off that easily.

"Won't the little girls miss you?"

"It's not the *little* girls who I'm interested in."

He was either forthright, brash, or a jerk and Sienna couldn't tell which.

"I'm sorry for intruding, ma'am…sir," he nodded to her and her father in turn.

At least he had manners, and a soft New England accent. It wasn't Massachusetts or Maine but might have been New Hampshire or Vermont.

"But I just have to know who you are." And he aimed his powerful smile at her as if it would melt her knees. Well, Sienna was made of stronger metal than that.

"The Goddess Aphrodite," she snapped at him.

"No arguments from me. Then you, sir, must be the Lord God Zeus to have such a daughter."

"Been called worse in my day." Her father's smile was not helping. Wasn't he supposed to be on her side?

Sienna glanced about the main hall. Though it was early, the museum was getting busier by the minute, yet they appeared to be in their own little bubble despite their proximity to a main staircase. It was as if the chattering families somehow sensed they shouldn't interfere with their small group. Above them hung the *Gossamer Condor*, the first human-powered airplane to fly a mile-long figure-eight course and to eventually cross the English Channel. It looked so frail, yet had achieved so much.

Frail had never been one of her choices.

"Sienna—" She turned and scowled at her father who stopped talking with a half cough-half harrumph before trying again. "My daughter finds your condition less than…impressive."

# # #

Roy smiled back at the man. Ramrod straight and clearly a soldier, Roy could feel him watching the crowd behind Roy out of habit just as Roy was watching the other direction. It made him feel a little safer. He also saw Julie was growing impatient with having to cover his simulator when she'd been headed on break—specifically a bathroom break.

"Well, sir, I find my condition less than impressive as well. It was a lesson hard learned about one of my…" he almost said 'fellow snipers,' but something told him that would open a whole different discussion than the one he wanted to have with the lovely Sienna. "Work buddies who I've already sworn on a bottle of aspirin that I will never listen to again."

Even her attempt at a sneer of disbelief looked amazing on her face. Her every thought was painted there, clear as day. And Sienna Whoever in a light blouse tucked into her pleasantly tight jeans had a body even more serious close up. Her combination of slender and curve was perfect in the way Jennifer Aniston's was—a bit of knowledge he could only blame on his big sister's crush on Chandler while they were growing up.

"I'm sorry, but I'll have to get back to my station. I simply wanted to ask if you," he turned fully to face her. He could smell her soap and shampoo and the gentlest hint of honey—too light to be a perfume so must be her. She was a hundred times more powerful up close than through his rifle scope.

She arched her eyebrows, naturally strong rather than studiously plucked, which he liked.

"If you would please have lunch with me today?"

Out of the corner of his eye, he could see her father—for there was no mistaking their having the same eyes and even the same manner of movement—watching his daughter. So, he too didn't know how to predict her next action. Independent thinker. Another plus. So many women didn't stand their own ground and left it to him to make decisions for both of them—which could get irritating as hell every time he made the wrong choice as if he had misread some secret code book.

The lovely Sienna would speak her own mind when she was good and ready.

"Fine!" Then her smile turned wicked. She tucked a hand in her father's arm and started off. "Fourteen hundred hours in the White House commissary," she called back over her shoulder, assuming that would shut him down.

He waited the beat so that she would think him stymied by White House security. Then he called after her, "I work here until then. Fourteen-thirty?"

She actually stumbled in surprise and barely resisted looking back toward him.

Her father's laugh told him he'd won that round.

Without a further glance at her fine walk—which he'd observed was very fine when she'd first walked away from him—he returned to Julie who was now mincing foot to foot.

"You owe me, Beaumont."

"I do, name your price."

"Lunch!"

"Sorry, I've got a date."

"Might have known," then she rushed off, leaving him surrounded by a milling hoard of happy, eager, short people bouncing up and down as they awaited their turn on the ride.

He and Julie had had some fun, but it had never gone much past some heavy flirting except for one night that had never been regretted, but also hadn't been repeated. Fun, but no spark.

He took a moment to watch Sienna the redhead and her powerfully built gray-haired father as they faded back into the crowd. Any fears he'd had about his abilities at target acquisition were gone. He'd be able to track her through New York streets at night if he could see a single lock of her lush, thick hair that must feel like—

A sharp tug on his jeans had him reaching down to lift the next boy aloft. His hangover was no longer as brain-piercing as it had been; the aspirin was finally kicking in.

Progress on many fronts.

#

Fourteen hundred hours slipped by as she delved into the implications of the latest reports on North Korean missile production.

Fourteen-thirty should have slipped quietly by while considering the completely different views of the Joint Chiefs and the Secretary of Defense regarding US force requirements in South Korea. The Chiefs wanted to push some of those forces into the South China Sea's piracy situation, also sending a message to the Chinese military buildup in the region. Defense, as far as Sienna could tell, wanted to take the fight to North Korea and turn the DMZ into the next Afghanistan.

But by fourteen-thirty-five she gave up all hope of concentrating. There was no way she was going to go out and see if there was some bleary-eyed docent hanging out at the White House gate. Besides, he was probably off having a three-beer lunch at his favorite watering hole. But her blood sugar had crashed a good hour ago and she wouldn't be getting any more work done until she'd eaten.

The commissary was quiet on a Saturday afternoon. The normal mayhem of weekday staff crowding the halls was gone; only a hundred or so hard-cores were scattered about the building. A cluster of Secret Service agents identifiable by their dark suits and coiled earpieces sat at a corner table to the back.

Several secretaries, looking no less harried than on weekdays but at least more comfortable in slacks and sneakers rather than dresses and heels, had gathered at a table in the middle of the room and were chatting happily.

She could envy them that simple circle of women. Her world had always been defined by men. Among her father's cronies—the pilots she'd hung out with at the HMX hangars where the Marine One helicraft were kept, and within the military she had come to know so intimately—women at high command levels were still the very rare exception.

She needed comfort food today and selected lasagna, a big hunk of bread with butter, a tiny plate of salad, and a bottle of juice.

It was only when she turned that she spotted him. Impossibly, the docent from the museum was sitting in the front of the room, close by the entry door but not where he'd be noticed if you weren't looking for him. His back was to the corner, setting him up to survey the entire room, but all he was watching was her.

His gaze was so steady that it drew her toward him until she ground to a stop just feet from the table. So steady that…

"Oh no! It's you."

He nodded happily, "It is. Nothing wrong with your powers of observation."

"The sniper on the roof," she wasn't in the habit of restating the obvious, but it just came out of her.

Again, his pleasant nod as if it was the most normal thing in the world for him to be here. His dark eyes were now clear and sharp, he'd shaken off the results of whatever excesses he'd imbibed last night.

"How…" No, that was a dumb question: sniper, who'd recognized her at the museum.

"Who…" Almost as meaningless: he was a Secret Service counter sniper. One of the most elite gunmen in or out of the USSS.

"Why?"

He kicked out a seat across from him with his foot. "Why don't you sit down before your knees let go and I'll tell you."

"Not the most courteous of men."

He shrugged, "Vermont born and bred. Don't see much point in doing the standing and bowing thing when it isn't called for. As Ma always said, I never was long on formal."

Somehow trapped by his unflinching gaze—if he'd looked aside for even a second she might have broken whatever spell he had cast over her, but he didn't—she settled into the chair and placed her lunch on the table.

"The way you walk, Ms.—huh, still don't have a last name for you—Ms. Sienna Aphrodite Goddess-of-Beauty, is an amazing thing."

If the next thing he said was what a fine ass she had, she was out of here. And as the NSA, she'd make sure he was reassigned somewhere far away and never came near her again.

"You walk as if you were more alive than any dozen other people put together."

"That's…not what I was expecting."

"Oh, I could remark on any number of other aspects to your walk that I expect would give you an excuse to ship me out—"

She definitely did not like being read so easily.

"But I rather like this posting, even before I saw how you could light up a day." And with no more ceremony than that, he bit into a monstrous ham sandwich that had been untouched as he awaited her, despite her late arrival. No matter how casual he wished to appear, he'd been sitting and waiting, too wound up to eat. Or perhaps too polite, despite his protests to the contrary, to start without her. Either way it was an unexpected and nicely flattering compliment.

"Vermont?" Sienna prompted him and took a bite of her lasagna making it clear she wasn't going to be the one talking.

"The Northeast Kingdom."

"Vermont is the size of half a postage stamp, how can it have something called the Northeast Kingdom?" She spoke with her mouth still mostly full, a habit she'd learned while standing too many watches beside the military she'd been studying.

"Clearly the lady doesn't know the true definition of a Yankee. Air Force brat?" he asked her.

"Marine Corps," she admitted. And all of the moving around that implied.

"Huh. Don't get a lot of Marines at the Air and Space Museum."

"Dad flew recovery helos on Apollo 11 and others," and she was giving out more information than he was. She didn't like it.

"So, you grew up mostly south of the Mason-Dixon Line, I suppose." He made it sound as if he pitied her poor lost soul for such a burden.

She took a bite of salad so that she had an excuse to restrict herself to a nod or she'd tell him a thing or two about Southern women.

"Well," and he settled back as if he had all the time in the world to tell a story and she didn't have a mound of reports already deep enough to hide most of her desk. "To anyone outside the US, a Yankee is someone inside. Inside our country, a Yankee would stake his claim north of the Mason-Dixon Line. North of there New England and in New England, a Yankee means Vermont. Oh, Maine might try, but they'd be wrong as could be."

"And inside Vermont?" He was obviously waiting for the prompt.

"Why someone from The Northeast Kingdom, of course." He said it as if it was a complete given.

"And inside the TNK?"

He snorted a laugh at her acronym. "Someone who eats Ma's apple pie."

"Which you do."

"Best in the world," he sounded ready to defend it to the death.

"That still doesn't tell me what the TNK is except a bunch of arrogant boys who can't cook for themselves."

Rather than protesting, he leaned back in. "It is the most beautiful place on earth. Green hills that roll all the way from sunrise to sunset. Trout in the streams just begging to be roasted over the fire. The woods smell of oak and pine and are deep enough that nothing but the birds or the deer will ever find a man."

"A poet," she teased him, but could picture it so easily.

"Spoken like a city girl," he teased her right back.

And he was right. Marine bases were big, busy places. And Marine Corps generals were not posted far afield. Suddenly she wished she could see his great Northeast Kingdom. Instead, she could picture the pile of work on her desk. It was—

"Do you shoot?"

The question was such a non sequitur that she could only blink at him in surprise.

"I see you drifting back to work and I see it worrying at you. Daughter of a Marine. Do you shoot?"

"Daughter of a Marine Corps *general*. Yes, I shoot."

"Christ. Your father is a Marine general? Surprised he didn't have me shot for hitting on his daughter."

"He…" No. She wasn't going to tell him that her father was the one who'd pointed this man out. "He knew I could take care of myself if I wanted to."

"Excellent. Let's go."

She looked down at her lunch, which she'd finished without noticing, and then back up at him. Whimsically, despite the fact that she was never ever motivated by whim, Sienna decided it really had been a crazy week and she could do with a break.

"There's no way I'm going to outshoot a sniper."

"I didn't say a competition. I was thinking more about unleashing some of those nerves hunching up your shoulders. They're awfully nice shoulders—one of those things I'm probably not supposed to be commenting on," and his tone told her there were many other implied compliments waiting their turns.

She wondered if they'd all be delivered so nicely. He'd skipped over the typical "nice ass" comment, only occasionally disguised as "you've got a great walk, babe." And if he'd looked at her chest, she hadn't caught him at it.

"You've got to relax if you want to shoot well," he slipped effortlessly back into the earlier conversation.

"I know that."

"Then let's go. We have a range just down the street a piece." He shoved back his chair and stood. When he turned to reach for his jacket was when she saw the big USSS across the back of his t-shirt, and the Glock tucked in a holster at the small of his back. Only the most trusted were allowed to carry a firearm inside the White House. Initially hungover or not, it said a great deal about this man and his integrity.

# # #

Roy spent the four block walk to the Secret Service building trying to figure out if this was real or not. Out in the July sunshine, she was even prettier than when sitting across from him. It was like she was powered by the open air even though they were walking through the heart of the city. It was so easy to picture her walking through the deep woods. Tipping her head back to breathe in the pine sap-scented air brushed as clean as could be by a fresh running stream nearby.

The more they talked, the less certain of himself he became.

Her White House security badge had annoyingly small print of her name. It wouldn't have been any problem pinned on a guy, but he didn't want to be accused of staring at her breasts while he was just trying to read her tag. And the woman never looked away to give him a chance to peek down at those nice curves, or the badge. While they'd been talking, he'd had a hundred percent of her attention which was so unusual that he could instantly tell when her attention had drifted back to work.

He'd blurted out the first thing he could think of to keep her attention, "Do you shoot?" How lame was he? Yet it seemed to have worked when he followed it through, making it up as he went.

The one thing he could tell about her badge was that it was the same as his: the rare "all pass." It gave her permission to enter both wings and the Residence of the White House. They were very rare outside the Secret Service and meant she was probably very high-level staff. Even cabinet members had to have a Secret Service escort when moving beyond the West Wing.

It irked him to know that if he'd been assigned to internal security, he'd have known who she was a week sooner, but he'd been on overwatch rotation and not included in briefings about staff changes inside the building. Then he'd been dumped into route planning with Frank Adams or some other high-end agent constantly hovering beside him. He learned more about route planning this week than in the entire year prior. He'd torn apart prior plans and reviewed future ones until he could see at a glance where the gaps were and how best to fill them.

But he still hadn't been briefed on senior level knock-out redheads.

She'd remained coy about her name and he didn't feel comfortable using her first name without permission, so he was stuck with the Goddess Aphrodite. He couldn't remember if she was love or beauty or something else. The longer it lasted, the more certain he became that he'd gotten it wrong and never should have crawled out of bed this morning. But he did enjoy working with the kids and it was a nice change from sniper duty. Then Sienna Aphrodite had slipped into his sights with her knowing smile and lively eyes.

Down the street, through the mirrored doors, and up to the front desk they'd talked mostly of the weather: the seasons of D.C., Vermont, and where she'd done most of her growing up near Marine Corps Air Station New River in Jacksonville, North Carolina. She was the first city girl he'd ever met who had thoughts beyond shops and parties and the status of this person versus that one.

At the security desk, he moved in to vouch for her as a visitor. She slid her badge across the desk and it was as if he'd ceased to exist.

"Greetings, Ms. Arnson," Marlene, who usually greeted him with the sharp edge of her tongue, was all smoothness and silk to—

"Wait! Arnson? That—" he pointed a hand helplessly toward the Air and Space Museum. "That was Brigadier General Edward Arnson?"

"Yes," she replied, deeply amused by some internal joke. "My father and I share that name."

"Shit!" He wiped at his forehead. "He's—" Then he clamped down on his tongue. Both Marlene and Sienna were looking at him with amused expressions. "Notorious." Notoriously strict and intolerant of anything that wasn't absolutely perfect about the President's protection. He and Frank Adams were two of a kind. Rumor had it that Arnson had turned down two promotions in order to remain in charge of the Marines at HMX-1.

And Arnson didn't limit his opinions to his helicopters or the Marines stationed aboard them. He'd never faced the man himself, but he'd heard stories and seen the shredded remains of USSS agents not living up to his standards.

Sienna was still smiling at him, as if waiting for the other shoe to drop. Sienna…Arnson.

"Oh shit!"

She laughed in his face.

He *had* been briefed on her, he'd just never seen the photo of the new National Security Advisor. "You're…" He stopped himself, but it was far too late.

Marlene was going to be spreading this story far and wide. If he thought the ration of shit Fernando and Hank had unleashed on his head was too much, he was in for a blood bath now.

He took a deep breath and looked down at her. National Security Advisor Sienna Arnson was awaiting his final reaction. But so was another woman, one he guessed was used to hiding deep in those liquid brown eyes.

"I believe," he drew it out just a little and saw the most tentative of smiles from the inner woman rather than the NSA. "I believe I promised my Lady Aphrodite a bit of shooting."

Her smile shifted. There was a distinct pause. Then, rather than going radiantly dangerous as it had on the first day when she was leaving the White House, it went soft and warm. That's how he knew he'd made the right choice.

In his peripheral vision he could see Marlene giving him a nod as if she didn't quite believe what she was seeing—Roy Beaumont actually doing something right.

He took Sienna's arm and guided her down the marble and granite hall toward the basement range. Once she was a half step ahead of him, he turned casually and stuck his tongue out at Marlene.

A dozen paces down the hall, Sienna asked quietly, "Did you enjoy doing that?"

"I did," he admitted. And would never again forget that the NSA missed absolutely nothing.

#

Roy led her down a long flight of stairs and through two sets of double doors, where they collected ear muffs and goggles before going through a third. The range had shooting bays separated by sound-muffled panels that also stopped ejected casings from pinging the next shooter along the line. Down a long, concrete tunnel there were ten targets hanging from wires. Some of them were a long way away.

Saturday afternoon was apparently a quiet time on the Secret Service basement shooting range. There were only three other shooters in the ten lanes.

The distance didn't bother her, but she was less certain about the man. Her position as the National Security Advisor had only knocked him off track for a moment. And he might be the first person other than her parents to see her as herself rather than the NSA or "some woman." She'd never, not until that moment in the Secret Service lobby, realized the difference herself. Yet when he had set aside her position and continued to treat her as the woman she'd been at lunch, her world had shifted just a little bit.

They visited the armorer.

"What do you shoot?"

"A…handgun?" How was she *supposed* to answer?

Roy sighed and took her hand. She couldn't ignore the easy strength of his big hands as he assessed her own. And it wasn't merely size he was interested in. He poked at muscles, flexed her fingers, even ordered her to make a fist around his two forefingers and squeeze hard before he turned back to the armorer.

"Let's try her on a Glock 43 slimline subcompact. I may be back for the 19 compact but I don't think so. Five magazines until we see how she does."

"What? Think I can't handle the big, bad gun?" What was she even doing here with him?

"No, I think it will fit your hand better and give you better control. You have medium hands but very fine fingers. It will actually kick a little harder because it's the same 9mm round, just less gun. I think you have the strength to handle that."

Okay, she was going to shut up now. He hadn't taken offense at her sarcasm. He heard her mistaken assumption and had simply corrected it. Why now, when her life was crazier than it had ever been, had she finally met a decent guy? These were stolen minutes. For the next seven months, she didn't have time for a guy, much less a decent one—jerks took less time to deal with even in a relationship. She was too busy, just like she'd been for the last—Sienna was not going to count the years.

He led her over to one of the shooting desks between a pair of the sound panels.

"Besides…"

And she already knew that smile. Here came the next compliment wrapped up in a tease. Oddly, she was intrigued to know how he'd pull it off this time. Then, for the first time, he very deliberately looked down at her chest.

"With your build, this is the weapon you'd want for a concealed shoulder holster carry."

"Are you saying my breasts are too small?" And then she knew that her unconsidered reaction was exactly the one he'd been counting on her having.

"Nope. I'm saying they're just about damn perfect and this is the gun to go with them."

Sienna didn't want to be charmed. He was talking about her chest like…like…like no one else ever had. She couldn't pin down what was up with Roy Beaumont. Then she could see him shift back into sniper mode. Almost like a cuckoo clock, this complete and total "guy" would stick his head out, tease her, and then duck away.

"This is a Glock 43. There's no safety as such. You—"

"I've fired a Glock before."

"Okay," and he backed right off. Even her father didn't do that. Roy took her at her word. Maybe she was the one he was driving cuckoo.

She checked the weapon was clear, loaded a magazine, and pulled the slide to chamber the first round. She could feel him watching her every move intently, but he made no comment.

The target looked to be fifty feet out, a third of the way down the deep range. The outline of a man with two sets of bullseyes on him: one on the face, the other centered on the chest.

The lane was clear.

She raised her weapon and sighted down the iron sights through her dominant left eye and—

"Hold it." Roy stopped her before she could move her finger alongside the barrel onto the trigger. "Keep your finger off the trigger."

Which was exactly where she had it placed, alongside the barrel rather than through the trigger guard. *Don't touch the trigger until you're ready to fire,* one of her father's lessons. *And don't draw the damn thing unless you intend to fire it.* Another one.

Roy then began to handle her. He kicked one foot to set her stance a little wider. Hands on hips to twist her slightly more to the side. He worked his way up her body and then out her arms making tiny adjustments. Sometimes he'd move something, like her elbow, back and forth until he was sure she could feel the difference.

Last was her head. Without taking the least advantage, his fingers slid into her hair and shifted the angle of her head tilt ever so slightly. It was a gentle, intimate gesture. One she could easily imagine leading to other places that she hadn't gone in far too long. Three years working the US Commands had elicited a lot of offers—very few of which had been even interesting enough to consider as she'd had so little time for extracurricular activities.

"No, leave your shoulders where I put them. You're raising them up again."

He left her to slowly find the position he'd set her in rather than laying his hands back on her and making the adjustments himself. She considered not returning to the initial position just so he'd have to put his hands back on her, which was too lame for words.

Besides, she could feel when everything settled into the "right" position. There was a cleanness to it—at least it was the best word she could find.

"Now, don't hold your breath when you fire, just pause for a moment before each squeeze on the trigger. Go when you're ready."

She liked the feel of the smaller Glock 43, the way the butt nestled neatly against her palm—once Roy was done adjusting her grip. She could feel the straight line of wrist, elbow, arm, and the solid support of her other hand cupped beneath the gun and her hand.

Sienna considered showing off, firing a fast series of shots like those she heard battering away in other lanes, but something about Roy's presence…she wanted to do her best. She squeezed off the first round.

No comment.

Another.

A whispered, "Don't adjust left, but *think* left. That will be enough correction."

She thought left and sent the rest of the magazine after the first two without eliciting any other comment—one per breath. There was a peace inside her as she made sure the weapon was clear and set it on the shooting desk.

Roy pressed a button and the chart flapped backward as the overhead wire pulleyed it to them.

"Nice shooting. Your father trained you well."

She did her best to ignore the two shots out in the five ring to the right. An eight, two nines with one just catching the edge of the bullseye, and one fully in the black of the ten. Ignoring the first two, it was one of the best groups she'd ever shot in her life.

"He never taught me the sort of things you did," she tipped her head and shifted her elbow to demonstrate.

"Different weapon. He probably ran you mostly on his Sig Sauer P226. And the Corps teaches differently. I gave you the base position we start recruits in. You build stance variations from there." And he lifted her empty gun, which looked silly in his big strong hands, and demonstrated a slow turn. The muzzle of the weapon never wavered that she could see, but his shoulders, hands, and head position shifted as he rotated from chin over his left shoulder to chin over his right. He then dropped to a squat and did the same thing, but the shifts were more dramatic.

It was easy to forget that something so apparently simple as firing a sidearm was also so complex. He made it look easy. This was Roy's specialty and he would be far more skilled in this arena than she was—or her father, which was hard to admit.

"Besides, the P226 is a lot of gun with a heavy round and would require a slightly different stance. I'd wager you hurt here after shooting it," he poked a finger into a shoulder muscle she knew all too well from past experience, "and the slide sometimes caught you here." His fingertip drew a line of fire across the webbing between her thumb and forefinger.

"Okay, Mr. Smarty Sniper. Show me your stuff." She needed a moment to recover from the unexpected intimacy of him knowing things about her body that only she should know.

She hit the "Out" button and sent the target flying back down-range. She didn't stop at the fifty-foot mark.

"Hey!"

Sienna kept her thumb down on the travel control.

"C'mon! I don't have my rifle here," he whined as it passed the hundred foot mark. She ran it right to the back wall at fifty yards.

"Head shots only. And your grouping had better be at least as good as mine."

"Blindfolded with my back turned and no mirror?"

"Maybe next time. This time I'll let you off easy."

He set down her empty Glock 43 and pulled its much bigger brother out of his back holster—a Glock 21 that fired .45 cal rounds. There was a weapon that looked proper in his hands. The fearsome warrior now stood before her in all his lethal might. Damn, but it looked good on him.

She stepped aside to give Roy room. He'd taken a minute or two to get her positioned.

It took him less than five seconds. He just went…quiet. Not frozen, but so still she suspected a deer could walk right by him in his precious Vermont woods without being disturbed.

The shots came impossibly close together. No, she caught the rhythm of the last few. She had fired once per breath, he was firing once per heartbeat.

He stopped at six, which came all within the same caught breath for her. Then he punched the "In" button before dropping the magazine and clearing the chamber.

"Same number of rounds to be fair."

The target arrived. Every shot was in or touching the much smaller black bullseye of the headshot except one.

"What was that?" She asked before she could stop herself. One shot had hit two inches high in the center of the target's forehead. The rest of his grouping would have fit easily inside the chest bullseye that she'd only managed to really hit once, and his was at three times the distance.

"Number three," he sounded ticked. "I typically drop the first two in the center of the chest and then shift for the head for the next two. I remembered a moment too late that I was already at the head and you had specified only head shots. So it went high. That high on the forehead, it might easily glance aside of the bone without penetrating the skull."

"That's amaz—"

Somewhere down the lane a series of shots rang out so fast she could barely separate them. It wasn't machine gun fire, but it was impossibly fast. Either two per heartbeat or someone with the pulse rate of a hummingbird.

There was a soft but heartfelt, "Damn it!" from the same direction.

A few seconds later there was another impossibly fast barrage, this time without the curse.

Two targets that had been against the back wall at the far end of the shooting gallery as Roy's had, started winging their way forward.

Roy leaned back to look down the gallery and then gathered up both of their weapons and the small pile of magazines. "C'mon. This should be good."

They arrived at the same time the targets did.

Sienna focused on the targets first. One had a lot of holes in the black at the center of the chest, one through the neck, and the rest inside or touching the black of the head bullseye. The other had near perfect groupings in the two blacks without any strays.

"Getting sloppy in your old age, Beat." The speaker was looking over at the target with the neck shot. She was a short but very shapely woman with Eurasian features and a streak of bleached blond in her dark, chin-length hair.

"Still a spine cutter, Kee." The first shooter—who had apparently been the one to curse after her round—was an equally powerfully-curved woman with dark, dark skin and just the first hint of gray in her black hair. She tapped her stray shot with the tip of her handgun.

Sienna had to swallow hard at the thought. These two women were shooting to make sure that the person wasn't just stopped, but stopped dead. Just like Roy shooting chest then head. They were talking about cutting the spine to stop an assailant. She knew *of* this world, but not about it. No matter how much she'd studied, she'd never been in a war zone, never had to shoot a live person.

Then a big, deep voice back down the gallery boomed out, "Who the hell shot this piece of crap?"

Sienna winced just knowing someone had found her target.

# # #

Roy groaned. It shouldn't be possible. It was Saturday afternoon for crying out loud.

But when Roy looked, there he was as real as life. Frank Adams came striding up the line with his and Sienna's chart flapping from one of his big hands.

"That's mine, I'm afraid, Mr. Adams," Sienna admitted freely, showing not the least flinch of mortal terror. How did she do that?

"I'm not talking about the chest. It's obviously civilian and nice enough shooting for one. Wouldn't take much to make you a decent shot if you can already do this, Ms. Arnson."

Of course Adams had known who the hot redhead was, even the first day on the roof. It ticked Roy off that the answer to the mystery woman's identity had been glaring over his shoulder all week; not that Roy would ever have considered asking him.

"I'm talking about this piece of crap," Adams aimed a finger right at Roy's high number three.

"Was shifting for a head shot, forgetting I was already there." It was an awful admission, because it meant he'd made a shot without thinking about it. But it was the truth, so he said it.

Frank tipped his head down enough to look at Roy over the tops of his shooting glasses.

Roy wasn't sure what prompted him, maybe hoping for a laugh from Sienna. But for the second time in the same week, he talked back to the head of the Presidential Protection Detail. First he raised his right hand.

"I do hereby solemnly swear that I'll never screw up again as long as I shall live. So help me god."

"So help us all," Frank boomed out with the solemnity of a Southern preacher with absolutely no faith in his flock. He turned to his wife. "Beat, send down a fresh pair of targets. Send them all the way down."

Beatrice Anne Belfour was the head of the First Lady's detail and Frank's wife. She was also rumored to be even more lethal than her husband. Roy was just glad he'd never had a chance to find out.

The other woman he hadn't seen before, but there weren't too many top shooters named Kee. This had to be Kee Stevenson, one of the top snipers in the country. He'd heard she was working with the FBI's Hostage Rescue Team on loan from the Army's 160th Night Stalkers helicopter regiment. He'd hoped to shoot against her someday in a competition, but he'd never expected to meet her in the presence of his boss.

"Beaumont," Frank Adams voice snapped him back to attention.

"Sir."

Adams set down his massive Sig Sauer P226. Then pointed for him to reload both Sienna's lean Glock 43 and his personal 21. Then he waved to Roy's ankle.

Roy lifted his pant leg and pulled out the Walther PPK he kept there and set it last in the row. It was a weapon of last resort, rarely used beyond twenty-five feet. But Roy knew it intimately and could use it very effectively; it had been the concealed carry piece his dad had given him for his sixteenth birthday—James Bond's gun, though in a smaller .22 caliber—and he'd worn it ever since.

Adams snorted derisively but made him lay it down alongside the others. He probably wore a howitzer alongside one of his massive legs.

"Shoot the two targets heart left, head right, heart right, head left. Eight rounds from your and my gun. Four each from the 43 and that wimp-ass excuse you call a backup piece."

Roy wanted to protest.

Wanted to just walk away.

He'd brought Sienna here for a little shooting and mostly some flirting, never suspecting how good she already was. And how quickly she learned. She remembered the body-feel of each positional correction perfectly.

And the feel of her body.

It had almost killed him to take his hands off the soft curve of her hips once he'd touched them. The warmth of her shoulders, the lean strength in her arms, and with his hands full of her hair it had required more self-control than he knew he had to merely adjust her head then back away.

And now Adams was being a total bastard—just as he'd been all week correcting every little thing Roy did—and was trying to make him into some kind of a goddamn fool in front of her.

Well, it wasn't going to happen.

Roy braced himself.

He'd never tried such a challenge. .45, .357, 9mm, and .22. Four very different weapons from three different manufacturers. And it would be easier to shoot until empty, but Adams wasn't even going to give him that. He rocked up on the balls of his feet and then resettled his heels solidly.

He could feel the background fading. Adams glowering behind him. Beat Belfour's impenetrably dark eyes observing every detail and Kee Stevenson's almond eyes so narrow he couldn't tell what she was watching. Off to his right, Sienna Arnson, the general's daughter.

To his left.

Four weapons.

Two targets.

They were all that matter—

"Double time it!" Adams' harsh bark didn't penetrate Roy's focus beyond the content of the added challenge. "Fire NOW!"

At his shout, instinct took over. Roy grabbed the first piece. Adjusted for the Sig's weight and hard kick, then unleashed it downrange. Chest, cross to head, down to chest, cross back to first head. Repeat. Drop the weapon. Next. Repeat. Next.

With his final weapon, the lightweight Walther PPK, he intentionally fired a fifth round.

He didn't watch the approaching targets as he cleared all four weapons.

Beat didn't pull them down, she just let them hang there. He forced himself to look up. The holes were slightly different sizes in the paper. The heavy rounds of Adams' Sig rose slightly from one to the next—it was hard to recover the feel when firing so quickly—the last barely touching the top of the black. The heavier .45s from his own weapon held steady. The other groupings were more consistent as well.

Nothing was wholly off the black.

Except that final one that had gone precisely where he'd sent it.

He gathered up his weapons and headed back toward the armorer to turn in the borrowed Glock 43 and the unspent rounds. He signed for number of rounds fired and reloaded his own weapons.

The last round, the fifth from his .22, was dead center of the target's forehead. Exactly where he'd placed his third shot when shooting for Sienna. Right where he'd like to put a round in Frank Adams for making him do that in front of her.

He was a half block down the street outside the Secret Service building with no idea of how he got there or where he was heading, when a hand took his.

It jolted him back to reality. He'd know her hand anywhere—since the very moment he'd first touched it while assessing what weapon would be best for her grip.

"I'm…" Roy didn't know what to say.

…sorry my boss enjoys jerking my chain?

…sorry it was such a crappy first date?

Sorry for…he didn't know what.

"Roy. Just stop a moment. Easy. Just stop."

He stopped, but didn't know what to do next.

#

No matter what those two amazing women did, Sienna had never seen anything like what Roy had just done. And by the long silence with which the other three had looked at the two targets after Roy had finished shooting, she'd guess they hadn't either.

She guided him over to a concrete bench along the sidewalk and made him sit down. Sienna let him just sit for a moment. The afternoon sun on his face. The lazy Saturday afternoon traffic rolling by. They were a couple blocks back from the tourist mania, so the sidewalk was relatively quiet. A couple of pigeons came over to see if there were any breadcrumbs for the begging, but soon waddled off in search of more promising subjects.

"What was that?" She asked only when she felt him come back enough that he might answer.

He scrubbed at his face with his free hand, she hadn't let go of the other yet. Still he held his silence.

"Roy?"

"Adams hates me. Wanted to humiliate me in front of you. I'd say he did a pretty thorough job of it."

Sienna's specialty was assessing situations as they developed. And her gift? She was far more consistently right than those around her. She tried to keep it based on an immense body of research, but occasionally, she just knew. Her consistency had eventually earned her the respect of four of the six US Commands' generals. The other two had been hard cases like the Secretary of Defense so she'd learned what she could from them (some of it how *not* to command) and moved on.

The problem was Roy had the situation completely backwards, but there was no way to tell him that. Say it head on and he'd just deny it. Call her a fool.

It had been a test. Performance under pressure. Three top shooters observing Roy, and Adams must know it was her and Roy's first "date"—for she couldn't deny that's what it had become. She didn't have any misconceptions about privacy inside the security bubble that was the White House—there wasn't any. There was discretion, but there was no privacy.

Adams had seen an opportunity and grabbed it—to test Roy.

Knowing that discussing it head on wasn't going to get her anywhere, she came at him sideways.

"What do you know about the two women?"

Roy eyed her strangely for a long moment, but soon began giving her chapter and verse. He was careful to let her know what was fact and what was rumor. It was crazy how the pieces fit together in unexpected ways.

Kee had served under the Two Majors, as they were now called inside military circles. Majors Mark Henderson and Emily Beale had formed the most responsive and mission successful helicopter company ever within the already impressive 160th Night Stalkers. Roy didn't know about them, but Sienna had met Beale during the major's last days at USCENTCOM and never been so impressed by anyone, man or woman. Her replacement, Warrant Officer Lola LaRue Maloney was almost as amazing in her own way and the 4th Battalion D Company was still one of the go-to teams in President Matthews' black ops arsenal.

Beat Belfour, even though she was in the same service as Roy, he knew even less about.

"Woman is just so damned serious. Makes her scary as hell because you never know what she's thinking. She makes Frank Adams look like a teddy bear."

"A teddy bear who you metaphorically shot in the head." Now she could approach the sore spot.

"Yeah," Roy bowed his head down to stare at the sidewalk. "Only shot I've taken in anger since putting a BB into my big sister's backside when she was ten and teasing the crap out of me. Adams will never forgive me that last shot any more than my sister did. You don't suppose he won't notice?"

She couldn't help herself. It just caught her funny side. This big strong man, a one-man complete personal defense team, worried about shooting a paper target in anger, and doing it perfectly.

"I think," she managed between giggles, "he might...have noticed."

"I suppose," he finally smiled for the first time since they'd sat down, "that it was better than if I'd shot the target in the balls."

"Imagine the look on his face if you had."

And soon they were both laughing.

It was a good moment. Sienna's good moments were always on the professional side, but this was a good moment on the personal side—such a rarity that she wanted to wrap it up and cherish it carefully. The warmth of his smile. The laughter in his eyes—

Then he kissed her.

Everything else fell away in that moment: her need to console him, the nagging background worry of the unfinished work on her desk, how inappropriate it was for the newly-minted National Security Advisor to be kissing a near stranger on the D.C. streets. All gone.

Roy's kiss didn't allow thoughts of anything else to intrude. It was about a confused man and a woman who was wondering if she'd ever met such an honorable person before. It was about a woman who had only ever seen herself "as the job" and a man who somehow looked past that.

When she finally broke off the kiss, it was for none of those reasons, but rather because she felt so...full. Like she wanted to dance and laugh and sing and weep all at once and if the kiss lasted one second longer she might try to do all four simultaneously and simply collapse from the internal chaos of it.

Roy didn't pull away or apologize or do any of those typically male things. Instead he looked at her steadily and brushed a callused thumb along her cheek.

"Clear in your sights, Mr. Sniper Man?" Because his eyes somehow really saw her in a way she'd never known was possible.

"Clearest ever, Ms. Sienna Aphrodite. Say, maybe that explains it. Did you put one of those goddess-type spells on me?"

"No. Explains what?"

"Why I suddenly specialize in being an idiot in front of Frank Adams, of course."

She almost bought into it. Was almost angry that he was back to worrying about Frank instead of focusing on the best kiss ever created.

But then she saw that hint of a tease in his eyes.

"Frank Adams, huh? Okay. You want to think about him, go ahead. But I have news for you, Mr. Sniper Man."

"This should be good," he sat back and crossed his arms. Gods but he was so gloriously male and she couldn't resist poking at him.

"You don't get another kiss until you can come back and tell me something personal about Frank Adams and Beatrice Belfour." Besides, she absolutely needed a little mental distance here to understand what had just happened. Because the female in her, who she knew so little about, was ready to jump him here and now on the city street and the woman who she was needed to slow the other one down.

He just gaped at her.

"And it had better be something nice."

Chapter 3

Sienna, Roy was sorry to discover, was a woman of her word. He managed to talk her into going out for pizza on Sunday night—very relieved that she was a woman happier to dine on a sniper's budget than a senator's. But he wasn't allowed even a good night kiss before she slipped away in a taxi.

His plans to pump Adams for some detail, any detail, were foiled when Kee Stevenson was waiting for him in the Secret Service ready room Monday morning.

"You're with me," clearly this was going to be her idea of a hardship assignment. She looked as happy as a losing candidate giving a concession speech.

"No, I have roof duty."

Kee handed him a sheet of paper. "Do what she says. Don't screw up. Adams."

He handed it back and wondered if he should go wash his hands, just as he would after handling some dangerous viper. Kee didn't give him a chance.

"Bring your two favorite rifles. Let's go."

He grabbed the case for his JAR—after all, the Just Another Rifle was the bread and butter of a Secret Service counter sniper—and after a moment's thought selected the HK PSG1A1—a rifle he'd always liked. Kee eyed him as if now Roy Beaumont was the dangerous viper. Or perhaps as if for the first time, he was actually of interest. Unlike Sienna, Kee Stevenson was wholly inscrutable and he'd bet neither of his guesses was accurate.

They went.

He considered pumping Kee for information about Frank and Beat, but her silence was just as daunting as Beatrice Belfour's and he reconsidered his plan. He couldn't even find a gap in her silence to ask where they were going; he was just a piece of meat along for the ride.

They headed south out of the city in a standard black SUV. He wondered if it wouldn't be safer to move the President around in an unmarked five-year old Chevy rather than the massively escorted motorcade made up of distinctively black-and-tinted armored vehicles, but no one was asking him.

Instead, all he could do was look out the window and watch D.C. roll by. They headed south. If Kee Stevenson was working the Hostage Rescue Team, maybe they were headed to Quantico. Was he being transferred there?

That gave him a jolt. He wouldn't put it past Adams to shuffle him out of the White House for even speaking with the NSA. Normally it wouldn't bother him. Especially after only two dates and one kiss. Such a change of logistics wouldn't rate more than a phone call or maybe a text: "See you, honey. It was good to be with you, but just transferred out of state on no notice. Thanks. Bye." In other words good, but not that good. Actually, with a lot of his past relationships he'd have welcomed the excuse. But for some reason, being jerked away from Sienna Arnson did not sit at all comfortably with him.

He nudged and prodded at that puzzle as Kee drove south out of D.C. Abe kept his eye on the city from his high stone perch, not caring crap about Roy. And if there was any Jeffersonian wisdom waiting for him, it wasn't coming from the domed monument. Despite driving through the land of such greats, he ended up no wiser.

Sienna had gotten under his skin. And not just the way she looked or had abandoned herself to one of the gentlest and sweetest kisses he'd ever had. It had always seemed to him that he and women knew what they wanted from each other and just took it—hard heat fired by lust and not much else. Sienna, the woman behind her NSA shield, was soft and gentle at heart and had somehow burned herself into his system.

When he thought of her, it wasn't the kiss. It wasn't *just* the kiss. He remembered her laughing with merry abandon over pizza at his account of his Friday night lack of exploits with Fernando and Hank. Her insightful questions into his childhood had explained his path to being a sniper in ways he'd never thought about. And he could still feel her soft hand clasped against his own rough palm as she led him to sit on that concrete bench.

The problem came when he asked her about herself. If you needed an example of a conscious career path driven by sharp intellect, you got Sienna Arnson of Washington, D.C. It was as if the woman didn't exist separate from her career.

On the opposite end of the spectrum, Roy knew he wasn't a driven man. If you needed an example of someone who just happened to be able to handle the heavy math of advanced ballistics and was tough enough to survive every form of training they could throw at him, you got Roy Beaumont of northern Vermont. He figured his best attribute was being too thickheaded to know when to quit.

"Huh, what?"

Stevenson had made an unexpected turn. Quantico was still a dozen miles away when she pulled up to a security booth alongside a big hangar. A hangar surrounded by helicopters not airplanes.

"You got a one-track mind, Beaumont. Give me your ID."

"I'm a sniper. We're supposed to have one-track minds." He handed over his badge.

"Uh-huh. And that's why you're wearing a stupid-ass dreamy expression rather than even saying 'Good Morning'?" She rolled down her window and handed both of their badges to the gate guard. The Marine Corps gate guard.

"Always dreamed of being a sniper."

"You keep thinking that and I might as well turn this car around and dump you back in Adams' lap. Don't think either of you would enjoy that much."

"What do you mean?"

She took back the IDs and handed his over as they rolled through the gate. "I mean, if your goal is to be a sniper, you're already there. What's next?"

"Huh." He'd never thought about it, but now that she'd mentioned it, he had kind of been in cruise mode for the last year. He'd made White House sniper. Didn't get much better than that.

"You're never going to be Chris Kyle with a record number of kills, neither am I for that matter, even though I'm probably as good a shot."

Roy leaned back to think about it, but didn't have a chance as Kee parked and they carried their rifles—she toted an unmarked case, battered and scuffed with hard use—through the back door of the hangar. There were a dozen helos parked in here.

As his eyes adjusted from the bright light outside, he could start to see details. Like the fact that every one of them was painted in the distinct green and white of the President's aircraft. These were the Marine One aircraft and their cohort of flying guard ships. That meant—

"Well, looky what the cat dragged in," General Edward Arnson strode up in Marine Corps fatigues and a dark blue t-shirt with USMC emblazoned across his broad chest. He nodded to the rifle cases, "Mr. Docent showing his true colors."

"Um, yes sir." Roy didn't know what else to say. He'd kissed this man's daughter and had been hoping to do so again. Looking at General Arnson, he wondered if he'd still be alive by the end of the day, never mind achieve the impossible and find out something "nice" about Adams and Belfour.

"Show some pluck, son," Arnson slammed a sidefist into Roy's arm hard enough to rock him sideways. "Gonna need it if you're going after my girl. Ain't me you need to be worrying about."

And Roy would believe that after hell froze over and cactus trees grew in Vermont.

"What can we do for you today, Kee?" The general's rough affability softened when he addressed the hard-edged Stevenson.

"I called in. Frank Adams wants me to take Beaumont here aloft. Do some target work."

Which was news to Roy despite half an hour in her presence. He'd done some shooting from helicopters…and been lousy at it. Anything beyond a few hundred yards was impossible to nail because of the vibrations and air currents. As a sniper he thought about breath, pulse, wind, temperature, and could even account for the Earth's spin on long shots. But with no stable platform, it was almost impossible to make a clean shot. From a helicopter, it was a challenge just to keep the target anywhere in the scope.

"Beaumont, huh," Arnson was inspecting him again.

"Yes, sir, Secret Service Agent Roy Beaumont." So Sienna hadn't told her father anything about him yet. Was that a good sign or a bad one? At the museum it had been easy to see how close they were. Maybe they didn't discuss personal matters? Or—

"Seems a hole just opened up in my schedule. What do you want to start him in?"

And Roy knew he was screwed.

"Let's start him in a Hawk, General. Don't know if I can trust him yet to not drop his gear off a Little Bird."

"Hey!" But they both ignored him and turned to the Hawk and began chatting about a "young scamp" named Dilya, who was apparently the First Child's part-time nanny. Roy was struck by how little thought he'd given to all that went on inside the building he'd spent so many hours lying on top of. It was just…the White House.

"Jeezum Crow!"

Both Arnson and Stevenson turned to look at him.

He just shook his head and they turned back to their conversation. Here he was as shallow as a mud puddle on a D.C. summer day and he was interested in the National Security Advisor, one of the most highly connected power players in the entire D.C. scene? She was responsible for wrangling the Joint Chiefs, intelligence, and cabinet secretaries into some form of agreement and he was responsible for…peeking through a rifle scope.

Roy tuned back into Kee Stevenson's conversation to escape quite how small he suddenly felt.

"…I tell you that Beat and Frank understand my kid way better than I do. I'm half tempted to put a bow on Dilya and stuff her under their Christmas tree this December."

Roy nearly tripped on the flat concrete trying to catch up with the conversation.

"Too bad you love her so much," General Arnson commented dryly.

"Yep. Too bad," Kee Stevenson may have actually smiled, but if she did, it disappeared as fast as it had arrived.

"Take me about ten minutes to get the bird prepped," the general peeled off toward the cockpit.

"Take me about the same with this cargo," Kee led him to the big open door in the side of the helicopter.

Roy couldn't believe he'd just missed exactly what Sienna had asked him for. He might be way down the ladder from the NSA, but it didn't mean he didn't want to try for her.

He'd never met anyone like her.

# # #

Sienna knew it wasn't Roy on the roof the moment she arrived at the White House. The one atop the West Wing tracked her briefly and then swept away to look elsewhere.

The one on the Residence barely hesitated as his sightlines swept by her.

She had learned the rhythm of the overwatch changeovers and just happened to be passing by the Secret Service room in the West Wing basement when the relief snipers headed aloft. No sign of Roy.

It was a stupid, schoolgirl thing to do—one that she'd never done as a schoolgirl—but she found an excuse to catch the next shift change as well. She spotted a Latino sniper headed out—one who she could easily imagine being the infamous Fernando, introducing Roy to his "cousins" all over D.C.'s worst bars.

Before she could move in to ask about Roy, the Secretary of Defense stepped up to spread more of his officious misogyny all over her. It took a couple of hours to prove that, just perhaps, she knew more about how USAFRICOM mishandled black ops force requests than he did.

It was an example of asymmetric warfare with him; she couldn't bring the big hammer to such a small battle and expect to win. While it would be far easier to simply slap the facts upside his head, that would lose all of the future battles. Instead she did the whole pretend-that-he-knew-more thing until she could finally transform her idea into his. It almost made her nauseous. Thankfully, she'd already briefed the President on precisely this problem, so at least he would know the true source of the solution.

Lunch wasn't an option, as she and the Assistant NSA had to tackle Egypt's most recent problems with the falling revenue at the Second Suez Canal. The plunging price of oil had made it cheaper for cargo and oil vessels to travel around the Cape of Good Hope rather than pay the high tariffs at the canal. The Catch-22 was that Egypt needed to pay off their canal building bonds. If they defaulted on those loans, then there was an even bigger headache coming to an already unstable government.

By the time she next managed to look at a clock, Roy was already a couple hours off shift.

And he hadn't thought to come by her office to at least say good evening or offer to get her some dinner.

He had all the consideration of…of…the Secretary of Defense!

Well wasn't that a disappointment! She rested her elbows on her desk and massaged her forehead.

A knock on her door had her jerking her head up so quickly that her neck almost seized up.

"You—" But it wasn't Roy who she was going to set straight about the right way to treat a woman you had kissed as if you had invented the concept personally.

Instead the head of the PPD, Frank Adams, was standing in her doorway.

"Evening, ma'am."

"Good evening, Frank."

"Are you okay, ma'am?"

She slumped back in her chair, "I look that bad, huh?"

Frank offered a puzzled smile, "Someday some woman will explain to me how to step around that question without getting slaughtered."

"Not a chance. I did a pinkie swear at birth to never reveal trade secrets."

"Should have known. You just look like it's been a hard day and I'm guessing that your blood sugar floored out a while back."

"Good guess."

"Go home, ma'am. Get some sleep or you'll never make it past the first month."

Sienna eyed the piles on her desk, the long list of unread e-mails, several bearing unread attachments which would lead to unread…

"Maybe you're right."

"Trust me," Frank offered a friendly smile and she did her best to return it.

"I just wish—" And there was no way she was going to mention Roy to his boss.

"Ma'am?"

"Nothing, Frank. And it's Sienna to you?"

"Not going to happen, ma'am. But I will tell you as a matter of, shall we say, general interest, Agent Beaumont is out for special training. He's not on the grounds today or tomorrow."

"Oh," and that popped the balloon of her blood-sugar fueled anger at him.

"Matter of fact, I expect he's hurting worse than you are. If that makes you feel any better, ma'am."

Sienna returned Frank Adams smile, "It might, Agent Adams. It just might."

In the first five minutes, Roy had gone through a dozen stages of frustration until he became sure that he truly didn't know anything. Not one single little…

It had started when Kee Stevenson had told him to pull out his first-choice weapon. They were sitting side by side on the 60's cargo deck, their feet dangling just inches off the immaculate concrete floor of the HMX hangar.

The Black Hawk UH-60, when upgraded and painted with the President's green-and-white livery, was dubbed a White Hawk. Even the escort craft that never carried the President, like the bird they sat in now, was armor and weapon heavy. They also carried flares to distract incoming missiles and enough spotting and surveillance equipment to pin down the enemy from much farther away than most craft.

But it was still the same sized craft as any 60. As soon as he swung the forty-six inches of his JAR up out of the case, he snagged the tip of the barrel on the fifty-two inch high ceiling of the cargo deck.

"Lesson one about helos," Kee spoke in a drill sergeant monotone. "Never have a weapon too long to swing inside your available space. Pack that beast away. Pull out your second choice."

He pulled out the Heckler & Koch PSG1A1.

"The HK is a better choice for helicopter work because it's eight inches shorter with the stock folded so you snag it less until you're ready." Kee flipped open her own battered rifle case and slipped out her own weapon.

He hadn't known that's what she shot with. And that explained the odd look she'd given him when he'd selected it as his second choice. It had been a consideration that maybe, just maybe, this fool of a White House counter sniper was worth her time if he selected the same weapon she used.

"Bought this myself."

Roy was having a serious case of rifle envy. It was the exact same model as his own, and yet it was a wholly different weapon. She had the Schmidt & Bender 3-27, seven thousand dollars worth of scope he'd been dying to try out, but that wasn't it either.

Kee's rifle was well used; it had seen a lot of very hard miles and it showed. The polymer stock was worn smooth just where her cheek would rest. Every single finger position was outlined by wear-use. How many shots did that take to happen?

There was a shine to a weapon that was perfectly maintained but had run through so much service. And it had a new barrel. That meant she'd run about ten thousand rounds through the last one and had to replace it recently. How many barrels had Kee Stevenson worn out?

Roy shot a lot to keep up his skills, but it was all range work. Kee's rifle was a weapon of war.

"To successfully snipe from a helo, you have to add several factors to your shot. First let's talk about isolating yourself from rotor vibration."

Roy was too well trained to need to fire prone. He constantly worked his way through the positions from lying flat to standing without even a tree on which to rest the rifle in order to retain his shooter's flexibility. Kee started him through variations of sitting firing positions that he'd never considered.

"If your tailbones are on the metal deck, you may feel more stable and connected, but what you're actually doing is transmitting the cargo deck vibrations into your skeleton. Roll back on your ass just a little more."

He did, and didn't like the unfamiliarity of the position.

"That's it. If it feels all wrong, then you're getting it right. Keep working that until it feels normal. Any time you sit anywhere for the next few weeks, I want you off your tailbones."

"Now, let's start talking about pilot factors. You'll never get to fly with the best pilot ever, Major Emily Beale."

"Why not?"

"Bitch retired to fight wildfires and have children. Go figure. When she flew it was like you were sitting on bedrock. She could hold a helo so still it might have been built right there in the sky. Fly with Lola Maloney and she'll fish you across the entire sky—she flies like she's dancing."

"She any good?"

"Chief pilot of 5th Battalion D Company."

"I meant as a dancer," he said it because the 5D wasn't the stuff of myth, they were the stuff of legend. If this Lola was chief pilot for them, she was one of the best pilots alive, anywhere. And that Kee flew with the 5D…no wonder she was one of the best snipers going.

Their standards were stratospheric.

Kee eyed him closely. It was hard to tell with her narrow eyes, but she probably rolled them at him before she sighed. "Lola's a damn sight better than you, white boy. And you want a hot lady like the NSA, you better start taking lessons."

Roy decided that in the future, he'd keep his mouth shut.

General Arnson announced he was ready—Roy had been peripherally aware of the general preflighting the White Hawk. In moments they were aloft and Roy decided Arnson flew like he hated Roy. He aimed for the air pockets and slid sideways almost as often as he flew straight ahead.

Or maybe he was just messing with Roy.

Which with the way his day was going wouldn't surprise him one bit more than a dairy cow on the front stoop.

Kee clearly enjoyed proving he didn't know shit about his own specialty as a sniper. Frank Adams was the bastard who'd sent him to this punishment in the first place. A punishment General Arnson clearly enjoying handing out.

And Sienna Arnson was so far out of his reach that—

Well, this had better be the day his life bottomed out, because if it went lower, he didn't want to know about it. Then just as they were flying into the shooting range, General Arnson called out evasive maneuvers and twisted the helicopter through a complete sideways roll.

Roy almost lost himself and his weapons right out the open cargo bay door; might have if not for the monkey line attached to his flight vest and the helicopter's door frame.

The general's laugh attested that Roy had a lot more to worry about than just Sienna's opinion.

Chapter 4

*T*hey spent Day One busting me down."

It was Tuesday night and Roy had showed up with a bouquet of dahlias, take-out Chinese, and a pint of Ben & Jerry's Cherry Garcia—announcing "Authentic Vermont ice cream" as he'd pulled it out—just on the chance of her being in the building and having a free moment. Sienna forgave him every one of her evil thoughts from the prior night, told her secretary to shuffle her schedule for an hour, and closed her office door against the outside world.

The Chinese food had cooled off halfway, and tasted fantastic. The ice cream had warmed just enough that it didn't break the plastic spoon as she kept dipping into it. The flowers kept drawing her eyes almost as often as Roy's strong face. It was so expressive. And somehow it had been transformed over the last two days.

"I should have seen it as it was—classic training tactics. Break down all assumptions and habits so that they can then build up new techniques without tripping over the old. But being just a dumb jerk from the woods, I didn't see it until just this afternoon."

"What happened this afternoon?" Sienna didn't even bother correcting the dumb jerk comment. He struck her as naïve only about himself. Now he was more sure of himself and also seemed more certain that he was living who he wanted to be more than any man other than her father. He had a real need to protect and serve that he'd found a way to express as a sniper. A sniper who had impressed Frank, Beatrice, and Kee in addition to herself.

"Shot eight of ten in the black at five hundred meters from a hovering helo. Five of ten moving at fifty knots at three hundred meters."

The way he said it told her that was pretty spectacular. "What did Kee Stevenson have to say?"

"She stated I: 'had promise.'"

"She what! Why that stingy, cheapskate—"

Roy held up his chopsticks to stop her. "No, seriously, it's okay. Kee is so incredibly good that it may have been the highest praise I've received since the day Frank Adams allowed me on the White House team. She taught me to do things I'd been taught were impossible. But she found a way around them, I think she developed half of the techniques herself. It was just incredible."

And there was the change. It was like when a soldier achieved a hard-won promotion. There was a new confidence. And since his easy surety of himself had been what first attracted her to him in the museum, the impact was now doubly strong.

"However," Roy continued as he fished out another piece of massively over-breaded, deep-fried, and sauced piece of General Tso's chicken—did he normally eat such things?

She could feel herself gaining weight just watching him. Sienna had stuck mostly with the twice-cooked beef in snow peas and the Cherry Garcia which sort of defeated her own argument.

"I appear to have failed miserably on another front," his sad expression looked like only partly a put-on.

"What was that?"

"My personal quest," he was watching her intently.

"Your quest?" Something in his look was making her throat go dry.

"I almost found something nice about Frank Adams and Beatrice Belfour…"

"But," she had to prompt him.

"…but I wasn't paying close enough attention and I missed it. Something to do with Kee's kid."

"Dilya." Sienna hadn't met her yet, but had been warned that no warning would prepare her for the meeting.

"Dilya. Something about how Frank and Beat understand the kid better than her mom does. But I didn't catch what."

"Surely that's got to be good enough to—"

"Nope," Roy cut her off. "I got the ground rules straight from the National Security Advisor herself. Don't see going back on my word any more than she would."

Well, the NSA was regretting her challenge at the moment. At first she'd needed to keep Roy at a distance. Her attraction to him was so powerful that she'd needed to blockade it and buy some thinking time. Now she'd had some thinking time—in between the minutes of mayhem that was her life—she was no wiser on the subject of Roy Beaumont.

However, the way she was feeling about him had shifted in that time, shifted to an even stronger draw than she'd first felt. She poked at another too sweet saucy glob of General Tso's to distract herself, but with Roy Beaumont sitting just across the table, it wasn't working. Somehow he had gained confidence without gaining arrogance.

"Well," she glanced at the clock and winced. She had a long night ahead of her no matter what advice Frank Adams had given her. But the clock gave her another idea.

"The way I see it, you have another twenty-five hours to complete your research."

Roy glanced at his watch, and she was amused to see him spin the outer dial to mark the deadline before glancing back at her. He didn't ask, he just waited.

She wasn't going to be that easy, and bit down on her General Tso's. Life would be so much better if fat and sugar didn't taste so good.

"Okay, I give. What happens in twenty-five hours?"

"In twenty-five hours I'm attending a reception for the new French ambassador in the Residence."

"Which means?" She was relieved when he took the last piece of chicken from the white take-out container, because then it would no longer be tempting her. She waited until he'd almost bit down on it.

"Because I'm allowed one guest. And if you want to get lucky, Mr. Sniper Man, you'd better have your answer lined up by the time you escort me to the reception."

He froze with the ball of chicken just inches from his mouth.

"You want me to be your date at a Residence reception?"

"No. You're going to do that anyway. You need an answer if you want a chance to get lucky *after* the reception."

He continued to stare at her completely goggle-eyed.

He didn't even flinch when the last piece of General Tso's slipped out of his chopsticks and landed in his lap.

Sienna didn't even try to hide her smile as she dropped her final question.

"You do own a suit, don't you?"

His nod wasn't all that different from one a bobble-head doll might have made.

# # #

Roy tried to delay getting dressed at the end of the shift. After a day back on the White House roof, he began to understand just how much Kee had taught him. He saw the city through different eyes, even though all she'd taught him was how to shoot better from a moving platform. The city now looked so still and…simple.

Which is exactly what tonight wasn't going to be. He'd wanted Fernando and Hank to be long gone before he pulled out his suit, but even that one wish wasn't going to happen. They got into some stupid game of hoop with a balled pair of socks and a small wire garbage bin.

Finally out of time, Roy pulled out the dry cleaning bag he'd smuggled in this morning.

He had their full attention in under three seconds.

"Yo, buddy! What's up?" Fernando three-pointed his socks into the top shelf of Roy's locker. "You disappear for two days with your rifles and now you be suiting up. Did you defect to a Protection Detail?" Any sniper worth his salt looked down on the guys in the close protection details. Those guys wore suits and fought with handguns and their bodies. A sniper belonged up in the sky making sure the guys on the ground stayed safe.

"Not a chance," Roy denied. "I've just got a dinner tonight."

"You sure ain't going back to Jake's Hole in that rig," Fernando plucked at his coat sleeve. Roy smacked his hand away and brushed at the dusty thumbprint on the charcoal gray of his only suit.

"I'm not going back to the Hole this side of ever." Even if Sienna walked away from him tonight, she'd given him another standard of woman to think about. One he'd never imagined before. Somewhere in the night he'd decided that if a woman the caliber of Sienna Arnson wanted to be seen with him, he sure as hell wasn't going to be the one to turn away. "It's just a dinner."

Hank grabbed the duty roster and scanned down it. "Only event tonight is some fancy over at the Residence. Don't see your name on the list. What gives, Roy?" Another drawback to having friends who were also in the Secret Service, they'd all been trained to hate unanswered questions. It had been drilled in so deep that it was in their DNA like an unstoppable itch until it was answered.

Roy finished changing and struggled with his tie, ignoring Fernando's telling him he should have bought a clip-on.

Still, there was no way he was going to besmirch Sienna's reputation with these jokers and if he had to suffer their questions, fine. But it didn't mean he was going to answer—

"Wait a darn minute!" Hank was staring too intently at the guest list.

Fernando had retrieved his socks ball and was once again going for the long shot into Roy's locker.

"The redhead. What was her name?"

"Which redhead?" Fernando wasn't really paying attention. He'd moved on to going for a bank shot off Roy's temple.

"Roy's redhead."

Maybe Roy would have been better off protecting Sienna's reputation if he'd just walked out of the locker room straight from his shower and attended the reception naked.

"Roy's redhead?" Fernando stopped and looked at Hank with a puzzled expression.

"Yeah. You know—"

Roy could see that Fernando didn't know, but the light of dawning comprehension on his face told Roy that making it two for two was too much to hope for.

"Roy's redhead?" Fernando said one last time looking at Roy aghast. "The new National Security Advisor?"

Hank looked down at the roster he still held in his hands, "Yep, she's on the list, as a plus one guest. Wait! You met the redhead?"

Fernando beaned Hank in the face with his socks. "No, doofus. How did you ever make the Service, huh? He didn't *meet* the redhead; he is her date. This dog is the 'plus one' of the National Security Advisor."

"Huh," Hank grunted as he processed the fact.

Question answered. Check. Next. Roy cringed and waited for it.

"Is she as hot in person as she is through the scope?"

Roy could barely remember the "hot redhead" walking up to begin her first day as the NSA, because she was so much more than that. But he had to rub it in the guys' face a little.

"Way, way, wa-ay hotter."

Fernando groaned as if he'd been stabbed in the gut.

Hank held up a hand to deliver a high five.

Roy raised his hand to receive his triumphant slap.

Someone at the end of the row of lockers cleared his throat.

Roy glanced over to see Frank Adams watching him with a look that said he'd better not be celebrating what he looked to be celebrating.

Shit!

He just couldn't catch a break in this outfit.

#

Sienna had fussed and worried about her dress. First she'd worried about overdressing, then about underdressing for the occasion. It was her first official White House reception for a foreign dignitary. Not being a head of state, the French Ambassador didn't rate a state dinner, but ambassadors did deserve formality.

If she'd been able to go in one of her business suits, she'd have been fine. But she'd invited a date. And that had started her down the path of dressing up for the occasion. Then a call to the First Lady's social secretary for any guiding tips—which Sienna had thought to be an utterly humiliating act to do, but had been very graciously answered. She told Sienna that dressing up would be *very* appropriate in no uncertain terms.

But she hadn't help clarify *how* dressed up.

Right before she melted down, a young voice said from the door of her office, "That's nice."

Sienna spun to look at who had spoken. And then looked again. The girl standing in the doorway deserved a second look. She was in her mid-teens. She had dark skin and an elegant face. She had jet black hair that cascaded past her shoulders in a smooth ripple.

There was a friendly openness to her face, but the captivating feature was her eyes, they were the oldest eyes Sienna had ever seen. They were hazel and appeared to leap out of her face. She was defined by those eyes. They changed a very pretty teen into a gorgeous young woman. She was dressed in a simple black dress that left her long in the leg down to her black, ankle-high boots.

"You," Sienna smoothed her own dress for the hundredth time, "don't think it's too much?" It was discreet at the neck with an asymmetric draped collar, short-sleeved, and high at the knee. But she hadn't anticipated quite how well the forest green jersey clung.

"Are you bringing a date?"

"I am," Sienna said cautiously.

"Two thumbs up. You'll cook his brain but still be elegant. It's a win-win."

"Thanks." Now that Sienna had taken fashion advice from her, it seemed awkward to ask the girl's name, as if they were already past that.

"Kee said you might be melting down right about now."

"Kee sent you?"

The girl's shrug explained it wasn't that simple.

And that told Sienna exactly who this was. Kee's adoptive daughter, Dilya Stevenson, the First Child's nanny.

"You need this," Dilya came into the room, undoing a small silver brooch she had pinned by her left shoulder. Without even asking permission, she came up and added it to Sienna's dress.

"What is it?" A four-footed animal with a big snout of some sort.

"A honey badger."

Dilya waited for a reaction, but Sienna didn't know what it was supposed to be.

"It's a symbol of strength—small but fierce. Just remember, 'Honey badger don't care.' If the nerves get you, just remember that. You can look it up on the internet later, but you're out of time right now." And she headed for the door just as Sienna heard approaching steps.

"Dilya?" Sienna called out and the girl turned. "Thanks," she rested her hand over the tiny pin.

"Sure thing," then Dilya whispered across the room. "Remember, 'Honey badger don't care.' Got it?"

Sienna shot her a thumbs up just the moment before Roy strode into her office as if he was out walking his grand Northeast Kingdom. He was…astonishing. Some men looked better in a suit, some worse. Some suits wore the man, so that the man disappeared behind the impression of fine tailoring. Not this one. Roy Beaumont absolutely wore the suit. His ruggedness wasn't transformed, rather it was counterpointed, making him look twice the man she'd thought him.

He strode right past Dilya as if he didn't even see her. He stopped only inches away from her.

"You," Roy spoke barely above a whisper, "are absolutely, knock-me-down gorgeous in that dress, Sienna."

Sienna could see Dilya's smile and two-thumbs-up gesture before she slipped out of the room.

She wasn't sure how he could judge her dress, because his eyes had been riveted on her face the whole way across her office. Now he stood so close that his face filled almost her entire field of vision. She wondered if she was about to have the crap kissed out of her, which would totally screw up what little makeup she'd applied.

His look said it was a very close thing and she figured it would be worth the price and then some.

Then he glanced down every so briefly and burst out laughing.

"Can't even compliment a girl and keep a straight face?" Her pride came prickling to life like—

"First, you left *girl* way behind. Hell, you look so amazing that you left woman behind too, except then I don't know what you are. I do know you're scaring the crap out of me, that's why the pin is so damned funny. 'Honey badger don't give a shit!' Indeed."

"I," Sienna swallowed hard trying to process the compliments, "I heard it differently."

"There's this video—"

"So, I've been told."

"Watch it and you'll get even more why you scare the crap out of me."

Sienna rather liked the idea of scaring the crap out of a man like Roy. "Are you planning to kiss me?"

"Haven't found the answer to your question yet or you bet your ass I would be. Sorry," Roy glanced aside for the first time. "I'm not really drawing room material."

"Are you trying to bow out?"

"Not if you're going to be wearing that dress the rest of the evening. I want a chance to look at you in it some more."

"How about if I offered you one-time, special dispensation on that kiss?"

"Nope. Lady set a challenge. Besides, the way I figure it, the night is still young. Give me something to do while all of you head cases are doing whatever it is you do at these things."

As if she knew. Again Sienna fought against being charmed and barely managed to hold ground. "Maybe you should have just asked Dilya yourself."

"Kee's kid?"

Sienna nodded.

"All I know is her name and that she was some starving orphan from Uzbekistan who now has full clearance all the way to the Oval."

"Really?" That pretty teen could just walk into the Oval Office?

"Buddies with the Main Man himself, according to the briefing docs."

"She was just here."

"She was?" And Roy looked about the room in bewilderment. He'd been so focused on Sienna that he hadn't even seen someone else was in the room when he arrived. That tipped Sienna right over the mush line.

"It's time for us to go," or she was going to kiss the crap out of him no matter what he said. As she turned for the door, he rested his hand ever so lightly on her arm.

"Just one thing first." He reached into a pocket and pulled out a small plastic container. "I figured a corsage might be excessive, but I hope you like this."

It was a single, miniature, yellow rosebud, on the verge of opening.

"Do you always give flowers to your dates?"

Roy harrumphed in thought. "Can't say as I do. Guess you're a special occasion."

"Well, free tip for you: Don't stop," she couldn't remember the last man to bring her flowers.

He reached out to pin it to her dress, hesitated, cursed, and then tried again.

She left him to be totally flummoxed by how to pin it in place.

He finally slipped the fingers of one hand inside the neckline of her blouse. His knuckles brushing along her collarbone stole her breath with the power of the simple contact. He quickly pinned the rose close beside the honey badger, then slid his hand free as if it had been burned.

"Best I can do," he said roughly.

She looked down to see that he'd pinned the rose so that the honey badger appeared to be sniffing it. Or maybe it was about to eat it.

"It's perfect, Roy. Thank you."

Then he offered his arm. She slid her fingers around his elbow, felt the strength there of a man who trained hard. She felt safer than she expected, than she'd ever thought possible for her first visit to the Residence.

She didn't need a honey badger or a rose, she had Roy Beaumont at her side.

# # #

Roy had done the math.

He'd been with the White House Counter Sniper Team for just over a year. Call it fifty weeks because of the two weeks he'd taken off to join his dad for the opening of hunting season and several weeks for periodic refresher training. He'd spent approximately half of that time on the roof and the other half on the unending daily crap work of being in the Secret Service (or trying to get warm between the winter watches). Roy had laid atop the Residence for roughly a thousand hours.

For the first time he was standing precisely twenty-seven feet below his normal post. And that twenty-seven foot decrease in altitude was one of the most terrifying things he'd ever done.

He knew most of the people in the room, either because he'd been briefed on them and watched them from his perch as they transited the White House grounds or he'd seen them on television just like the rest of America. He knew a total of three people in the room: Frank Adams, Beat Belfour, and his date. He'd been introduced to the White House Chief of Staff once, but that didn't count because the man wouldn't remember—

"Hello, Roy. Glad to see you again." Daniel Drake Darlington III held out a hand and Roy shook it out of pure relief. The Chief of Staff's hand was strong. He sported weightlifter calluses which was more than most of these soft, political men. It definitely counted toward Daniel's credit.

"Very kind of you to remember, sir." It was stiff and awkward, but it was all he could muster.

"A bit of a change from overwatch."

Roy looked for any hint of an insult, as if Roy was an unwelcome intruder from some lower class, but everything about Daniel appeared genuine. Rumor stated that he was a genius and one of the kindest people in D.C. Maybe both were true. "Takes my breath away, a bit, sir."

"Daniel," the Chief of Staff insisted.

"That will take some getting used to as well, sir."

"Doesn't it though."

And for that Roy swore he would try to loosen up around the man.

Daniel turned to Sienna, "Welcome to the Residence, Sienna."

"Thanks, Daniel." There was an easy familiarity, though Roy noticed that her voice was little more than a hoarse whisper even if the Chief of Staff didn't.

Daniel was pulled away as Roy glanced down at her. Her pale white skin, which made her brown eyes such a visceral shock, was tinging blue. He leaned over until his mouth was close by her ear and his nose was practically buried in her hair, "Breathe!"

"You first," Sienna joked, but managed to start breathing again.

He was momentarily mesmerized by the movement of her chest as she breathed deeply several times, but managed to shake it off before she noticed.

That dress had been messing with his mind since he'd pulled his own suit out of the back corner of his closet. Imagining Sienna out of her Washington-dulls and dressed up had been hard to formulate into an image, until the very moment he'd stepped in at her office door. The breath had been knocked right out of him. Snipers were trained to capture an entire image and then process it while ducked back in safe hiding.

That first, full-length glance of Sienna Arnson dressed to dazzle had done just that and it still was. Though she stood close beside him, he could still visualize every single detail of how she'd looked as he'd entered. Smiling, happy, and drop-dead gorgeous. She made him feel as if he'd been smacked upside the head like… like a squirrel that had jumped off a high branch and missed the next tree only to thud down onto the pine needle-strewn ground. He needed to go lie in a field somewhere until his head stopped spinning.

Sienna out of her Washington-dulls and in a cocktail dress—at least he suspected that's what it was called—was revelatory. If he'd been gobsmacked by the National Security Advisor, he was blown out of the water by the woman revealed. And the neckline that exposed just the very first rise of her exceptional breasts was giving him a great deal of trouble—they weren't over- or under-sized, they were just exquisite. The dress teased and enticed, invited a man to look and imagine. And those thoughts led down to a trim waist defined by curvy hips. Her legs, he really wasn't going to think about those legs, because they were—

He tore his attention away and back to the room before he forgot how to breathe.

"The room may be daunting, but the fantastic way you look isn't helping matters," he muttered softly to her.

"Really? Cool!" She sounded far too pleased and vowed to never speak again.

They were both still rooted in place at the entrance to the main hall of the second floor of the Residence. They had ascended the Grand Staircase together rather than taking the elevator and been just fine as they crossed the intricate parquet floor to stand in the archway that opened onto the Central Hall.

The hall was a dozen feet high, twenty wide, and stretched for about a dozen miles down the entire length of the Residence. The last colors of sunset filled the giant half moon window at the very far end with bold oranges, deepening to red even as he remained riveted in place.

The room's carpet was white, the furniture rich green leather with dark wood, and the walls the palest yellow. There was a grand piano, potted trees, and a half dozen of his fellow agents posted discreetly along the walls. The doors to either side led to the Yellow Oval Room and the First Family's private apartments. This President didn't live on the third floor. Rumor said he wouldn't even set foot there since his first wife's death—for they had been her private apartments. Hearsay stated that he hadn't been up there while she was alive either, but Roy hadn't joined the White House detail until after Geneviève Matthews was already the second First Lady. Now Daniel and his wife lived upstairs, the first Chief of Staff to do so in many decades.

But all of that wasn't what defined the room. It was the half a hundred people circulating in the massive space who made this not just another overly fancy gathering. The power elite of

Washington, D.C. filled the room. Daniel, the Vice President, and the President, all accompanied by their knock-out wives. The Chairman of the Joint Chiefs of Staff in full uniform—and General Brett Rogers who had been a Special Ops soldier for decades and had the battle ribbons to prove it. Cabinet members, congressional leaders…it was a daunting array for a mere sniper to be caught in.

There was conversation and laughter, serious circles of discussion and casual ones, men in expensive suits and a stunning array of women in amazing dresses—some of whom really shouldn't be, but some of whom absolutely deserved to wear such attire.

He'd seen Sienna checking her dress in the occasional mirror as he'd escorted her to the Residence. She didn't have a single thing to worry about.

And still both of them remained riveted under the stairway landing's arch.

"Sienna?"

She looked up at him wide eyed, her chest still moving a little too fast.

"Don't hyperventilate on me."

"Why?" She actually gasped a bit. "You think fainting would be bad form at my first White House party?"

"Screw that. You faint and I'm stuck here with these people by myself."

"What? You wouldn't just sweep me into your arms and take me away from all this?" Her breathing sounded a little more normal.

"Hmm," Roy considered the scenario. "I can work with that. Go ahead. Faint away and I'll get us both out of here pronto."

"Remember what honey badger says," someone whispered from close behind him. Then, before he could turn to fully see who it was, he felt a sharp push in the center of his back. A long slip of a dark girl faded sideways into the crowd.

"Who was that?"

"That," Sienna managed as they now moved slowly toward a nearby knot in the crowd, "was Dilya Stevenson. She gave me the pin."

Roy looked around, but she'd disappeared somewhere. When he focused front, there were the President, the First Lady (who was at least as beautiful in real life as the magazines made her), and a couple he didn't recognize. He'd guess they were Mr. and Mrs. French Ambassador—correction, Mrs. and Mr. French Ambassador as the title was hers, not his. Roy felt a slight rearward tug on his arm of Sienna slowing.

"You've got no worries, lady," he told her when they were still a few steps away from the group. "You're the most stunning woman in the room."

She shot him a quick look of surprise and then he could see the NSA shield start to drop over her.

"Don't do that. Just be you."

It had been one of his dad's rare lessons from back when he was trying to figure out how to impress girls.

"Besides, Sienna Arnson is amazing enough to scare the crap out of me even without the honey badger pin. Bet she scares everyone one else too."

He didn't have time to see her reaction, because they'd arrived.

# # #

Sienna didn't have time to sort out her feelings about Roy's last several comments. Combined, they made her feel a little taller and a little stronger. Even so (she dug her fingers hard into his arm to make sure he didn't get away), Siena wasn't letting go of Roy's bulwark of strength and support.

"Good evening, Mr. and Mrs. President, Mr. and Mrs. Ambassador. May I introduce Roy Beaumont?" He did the nod and handshake thing, being effortlessly polite.

He thought she was beautiful, she'd heard that enough to know it was true. But that Roy thought her beautiful while they were walking up to the exquisite First Lady dressed in a long sheath dress of gold with an Asian flower design flowing up the front in soft lavender was utterly ridiculous. She'd have attributed it to his trying to flatter her, except Roy hadn't done that…ever. If he really was as straight-ahead a guy as his occupation implied then—

She flipped to her college French and did her best to ask if this was the ambassador's first visit to D.C.

No for her, yes for him. *Shoe is on the other foot, Mr. Husband to the Ambassador.* Of course the French were more open to powerful women. Then why had Roy told her to check her NSA persona at the door? It hadn't felt as if he was trying to put her down or box her in. Maybe he was just… Now was not the time to ask.

First Lady Geneviève Matthews joined in easily, her French fluid though with an unusual lilt that must be her Vietnamese upbringing. It quickly became obvious that Roy and the President barely spoke a word of it and were soon left out in the cold. But Roy didn't appear abashed and took it in stride as he did everything else.

She half listened as Roy made some joke about locking the First Family away in Fort Knox or with NORAD down under Cheyenne Mountain for the entire term of office. Rather than being offended, Peter Matthews was soon chatting about Roy's job with what sounded like genuine interest.

Sienna lost the thread of the French conversation at the President's amused comment to something of Roy's that she'd missed.

"You had Kee Stevenson drag you aloft? Now that is one tough woman."

"Noticed that myself, Mr. President." Roy didn't look at all surprised that the President knew Kee. As if it was so normal for the Commander in Chief to be hanging out with military snipers.

"You met her kid yet? She takes after her adoptive mother with a vengeance."

Roy glanced in her direction, as if to make sure she heard what he was about to say next.

"Is that why Kee wants to give her away to Frank Adams and Beatrice Belfour as a Christmas present?"

The President laughed easily, "Two hardcore agents who never had kids didn't stand a chance around Dilya. I mean that girl has us *all* wrapped around her little finger, but Frank and Beat dote on her as if they were her grandparents even if they aren't old enough to be."

Sienna could see the look of smug victory on Roy's face. He'd found out something nice about Frank and Beat and obtained it from the most unimpeachable of sources.

"I knew it," Dilya's voice sliced right into Roy's smug expression. She'd come up behind them, carrying a two-year old who was the spitting image of her First Lady mother. The toddler's dress was a luminous gold to match her mother. It also served to accent how nice Dilya looked in her elegant black.

"Knew what?" the President asked.

"These two," Dilya nodded at Sienna and Roy. "Something about Frank and Beat. Like they've been scheming on it."

Sienna could see that somehow Dilya knew exactly what was going on, no matter how impossible that was. In fact, she was clearly enjoying outing their little conspiracy to the President.

"No," Roy stumbled out. "We just…" But he had nowhere better to take it than Sienna did because they had indeed been scheming. Scheming on how he was going to get a second kiss tonight. And at the rate he was going, a whole lot mo—

"Let's get to the bottom of this." The President barely had to raise his hand for Frank to materialize at his side. If Roy's height and strength had made her feel safe, Frank's breadth of shoulder overshadowed even the personal power of the President. He became the dominant force of the group, probably of any group he was in.

Oddly, Roy didn't fade.

Sienna was used to judging and working with power dynamics in a group, and it was a close thing between Roy and Frank as to who was the more impressive.

The President glanced around and also caught Beat's attention. In a moment, she joined her husband.

"Mr. Beaumont here wants to know why you two never had children of your own that makes you so dote on Dilya?"

"No, I—" Roy tried to protest, but the President's broad wink shut him down.

Dilya squawked as well and only looked a little quelled by the President's, "Hush, you." Clearly her little plot had spun out of her control in a way she hadn't anticipated. Sienna suspected that few things did that to Dilya.

Frank Adams cast a baleful look at Roy that Sienna figured would have melted any lesser man right where he was standing.

It was Beatrice who laughed. "Because we love the kid so much."

"I do not think your answer," the First Lady stepped up, "is such enough to answer my husband's question even though he would hide it as Mr. Beaumont's." The First Lady took her daughter from Dilya's arms and hugged her close. The little girl started to play with her mother's hair. Sienna was charmed that Geneviève Matthews did nothing to stop the damage to her perfect coif, instead she turned enough to kiss her daughter on the nose.

Frank looked sad and Sienna wondered how she could rewind this so that the question had never been asked. Somehow go back to before she'd set the challenge to Roy. But it was too late.

"It was both of our faults, Mr. President," Beatrice answered soberly, resting a hand on her husband's arm. "I was out in the field, specializing in assignee protection in hazardous situations, as you may recall, sir. I loved it and didn't want to back away. But by the time I eased off—"

"I was the head of your detail by then, sir," Frank Adams cut off his wife who was having some trouble speaking. "I refused to be some absent father—as heading your detail is not a part-time job—who might have to step in front of a gun and cost my kid having a father. I was going to resign, but Beat wouldn't let me. She said this was too important and she was right, sir. Then she stepped in as the First Lady's head of detail and I didn't want her to give that up. It has been an honor."

Sienna's breath caught in her throat. Their impossible sacrifice was deeply humbling.

The President didn't even hesitate. He reached out and shook Frank's hand solemnly in both of his. Frank nodded and they were done.

Sienna heard the First Lady curse lightly under her breath, "Mens!" She shifted her daughter into one arm and wrapped the other around Beat and hugged her tightly.

"This one," the First Lady joggled her daughter, "is just starting on her terrible twos. Any time you wish to steal her, please do." Then she shifted from joking to intimately sincere. "I know of no one she would be safer with."

"Aw crap," Dilya's sniffle summed it up.

Beat shifted back into her serious, head of the First Lady's protection detail mode, which no longer looked as daunting as it had only moments ago, then turned to Dilya. "Kee loves you too much to do it, but if she ever cuts you loose, Little One, you know where you're always welcome."

"Yeah," Dilya sniffled again, hugged Beat, and then grabbed the First Child and practically bolted from the room.

Frank and Beat faded back into their discreet, watchful mode along the walls. The President and First Lady were swept up into fresh conversations and suddenly she and Roy were left alone in a momentary vacuum in the middle of the crowded hall. It had been as if an air space had been formed around them with the President, a space that no one else had dared to cross and the effect still persisted for a few moments.

"Do me a favor, beautiful," Roy laid his hand over hers where it was still tucked around his arm.

"Sure. What?" She wasn't surprised by the rough tightness of her own voice.

"No more quests. I'm not so sure that I like the answers."

Sienna could only nod in response.

#

The rest of the evening was a blur to Roy. He shook the hands of more people in the next two hours than he typically did in a year. He unearthed stories of the Vermont woods that had made others laugh…without knowing quite what they had said to make him tell each particular story.

He was only really conscious of two things.

First, the incredible safety of the situation. All of the back-stabbing knives in the room were sheathed in polite words, and he was fine ignoring those. Though some cabinet secretary, who made Sienna clench unexpectedly hard on his arm, was saved a quick thrashing by the sudden arrival of the Vice President. Even on his best behavior the secretary's manners weren't all *that* impressive. However, Roy decided it would be a poor tactical move to punch the man for his tendency to speak to Sienna's breasts, so instead he maneuvered himself to block obvious sightlines and avoided the whole situation.

Other than verbal forays, this was one of the most secure rooms at the moment, anywhere. And because the gathering was in the central hall, it would take a missile strike to have a chance of reaching them. A sniper never was on the front lines like the ground details, but somehow the twenty-seven vertical feet from his rooftop had moved him through some strange zone between "outside" and "inside" the Secret Service's protection.

The second thing that dominated Roy's attention through the evening was his infinite awareness of the woman who never let go of his arm. At first he was relieved because he didn't want to be caught alone in a place he so little belonged. When he realized that her attachment in turn was part of an unstated mutual protection pact, he didn't complain. Sienna wanted to be next to him so that she wasn't cornered by some jerk? Fine with him.

Her skill on the social battlefield was utterly daunting. People of all calibers had sought a few moments of Sienna's time. He didn't recognize what was happening at first, but it soon became clear. She had a view of such clarity about global situations, that they were coming to her for interpretation.

Roy often had trouble following their questions. After a while he realized that was because the inquirer didn't have a clear grasp of what they really wanted to know either.

Sienna's answers however, were crystalline. By the time she was done, both the inquirer and himself understood not only the intended question but also the situation in a new light.

The tension between the nuclear powers of India and Pakistan as seen through the lens of current Indian military purchases and at-home manufacturing efforts of military products. The delicate alliance balances among the vastly different countries in ASEAN, the Association of Southeast Asian Nations who had been enemies for thousands of years and were now discovering how to be trade partners. The…

Sienna's knowledge was encyclopedic and her insights laser sharp. She delivered them not as he would have, with a get-a-clue tone, but instead with a gentleness that he was rapidly learning was her trademark. A gentleness backed by an intellect too powerful to ignore.

But as the evening progressed, he found his favorite moments to be when it was just the two of them. That's when she relaxed and was able to tease him about not having worn a suit in over a year, and he learned more about what it had been like growing up as a girl with a military father. When he caught himself keeping a mental list of things he would and wouldn't do when he became a father, he practically choked on the beer he'd managed to scrounge up from somewhere amid all of the champagne and cocktails.

#

Sienna had managed to make her first glass of white wine last most of the evening. She'd also survived the evening, which she certainly wouldn't have without Roy's stalwart support. She'd worked a dozen years toward this goal without realizing quite what she was doing.

Her father's fascination with the strengths and shortcomings of the American military complex had become his daughter's. She'd double majored in military history and political science. And that was before her graduate work in socioeconomics and geopolitics.

She'd been too busy during her first week of being the National Security Advisor to realize she actually *was* the NSA. This evening had brought that home with a vengeance and Roy had been the only anchor that kept her from sitting down and whimpering in a corner. With each successive little "chat" she'd become more and more who she already was. It was a more powerful transition than her valedictorian speech at Yale's Jackson Institute graduation ceremony with her Masters in International Relations clutched tightly in her hand.

Sienna had started the evening deciding that survival was going to be ninety percent "Honey badger don't give a shit!" and ten percent Roy Beaumont. But there was something about the way Roy kept looking at her, and adding one of his straightforward, practical world explanations that illuminated particularly complex scenarios, that had her shifting that assessment. By the end of the evening she decided it was about forty percent Roy, twenty percent honey badger, and just maybe forty percent her as well. Their "cooperative dynamic" was both encouraging and intimate. But beyond that it was familiar and easy, as if she and Roy had been doing this sort of thing since forever rather than having met just a week ago.

A few people had left. As with any party, the first wave mostly included those who had grown bored through their own lack of popularity. She judged that she could perhaps slip away with the next tier of departures, which would include those with unfinished work or other plans for the evening.

Roy hadn't given her a single smug look about finding out a piece of Frank and Beatrice's story. Not one hint that by their "deal" there was a potential for something more happening between them this evening. Perhaps she understood. Roy was the perfect gentleman and what they'd found out about the heads of the First Family's two protection details was not grounds for any hint of smugness.

"*Excusez-moi.*" French Ambassador Magda Armand came up to them. She was one of those effortlessly elegant women. Several inches taller than Sienna, with a fall of silver-white hair. Her husband appeared a mismatch, ever so slightly round and frumpy despite his immaculate suit. He was now snoozing quietly in one of the armchairs with a book in his lap and an unfinished glass of port on a nearby table. For an instant she wondered how much Roy would pay to be allowed to do the same, though he'd shown no signs of wishing to be anywhere other than at her side.

"*Bonsoir, Madame Ambassador.*" Sienna's burgeoning thoughts of escape momentarily quashed, she became intensely aware of the fact that her feet were killing her. For any future parties she would wear flats, no matter what others said, especially if they were as elegant as the Madame Ambassador's.

"As your friend does not speak French, we will converse in English."

Roy bowed his head in mute acknowledgement, thoughtfully deferring to the fact that the ambassador had sought out Sienna. After so many years associating with the military and the commensurate male assumption that the man was of course the center of attention, Roy was still a constant surprise.

"You know of our security challenges."

Sienna did. "Generally open borders combined with being one of the most active allies in combating terrorist organizations. It has made your country a prime target."

"Yes. Precisely. My country would be very interested in hearing the insights of America's National Security Advisor on improvement of our borders' strengths. You very much impressed General Dumont while *vous étiez présent* at USEUCOM."

"I would be glad to speak with him at his convenience." And watch her jammed schedule force her personal life to disappear even further than it already had. Not that she'd ever really had one. Actually, with Roy, she'd glimpsed a sliver of hope for a personal life.

"The challenge, if I may Madame Ambassador," Roy spoke up, "is that your problem runs far deeper. Your government is seeking to create control in a chaotic world. In the Secret Service we create narrow slices of security, just wide enough for our heads of state to move safely through. Most state security that I've studied had been border-based and yet we are a global economy. I have sat for hours at airports watching the number of flights in transit through that one terminal at that one airport. Comprehensive border control is no longer a viable approach."

"You are with the Secret Service, *non?* Does your National Security Advisor need protection even in this environment?" The Ambassador made it a soft joke but there was interest behind it as well.

Sienna would have to say yes. Maybe especially in this environment—at least for moral support if not for any physical danger.

"It is my honor to escort Ms. Arnson this evening, ma'am."

The ambassador looked at Sienna for an uncomfortably long moment. "If I may be the advisor for a moment: do not let this one slip through your grasp."

"I'll try, Madame Ambassador," because how was she supposed to explain this was only their third date. Fourth if she counted Chinese food and ice cream.

"So, Agent Beaumont, what advice do you have for my little country?"

"I'm just a sniper, ma'am. You have people in your Ministry of Defence far more skilled than I am at these matters."

The ambassador continued to watch him and Sienna kept her mouth shut. Through the evening she'd learned that if there was enough silence, Roy would often step into it with an insight from an unexpected angle. Apparently Magda Armand had made a similar assessment during the times their discussion circles had overlapped this evening.

"Well," Roy rubbed at his chin. "I'm from Vermont and we hunt deer there. There was a particularly pretty doe that kept slipping away from me time after time. In the end I stopped doing what I'd always done: setting up blinds in trees to watch on high, tracking along fresh trails used by others, and the like."

"I see the analogy," the ambassador nodded. "How, if ask I may, did you finally capture your doe?"

"Oh, I didn't."

"What?" Sienna burst out. "Then what's the point of that story?"

And finally she could see that she, at least, had walked right into his trap. His smug, knowing smile that she'd been waiting for all evening was finally on show. There was a warmth to it as he turned to gaze at her with his soft blue eyes.

"I sat and waited for her to come to me of her own accord."

And Sienna realized that was precisely what Roy had been doing all evening. The perfect gentleman. The thoughtful date. The man who didn't push or assume. He had indeed watched her from "on high" atop the White House roof and tracked her from museum to White House to a Chinese dinner in her office. But tonight, after he'd won his victory, he had merely bided his time.

"As I say before…" the ambassador trailed off.

Sienna knew. "Don't let him slip away." She tightened her grasp on the crook of his elbow. After how little she knew him, it should feel abrupt. But by some odd series of events that eluded her, they had skipped past so many of the typically cordial and careful steps of early dating. She knew intimate things about Roy and he of her. They could be months into their relationship, if it had contained more than that one kiss.

"As to your problem, Madame Ambassador," Roy turned back to the evening's guest of honor, knowing full well that he'd left Sienna at least momentarily overwhelmed. "You must stop doing what you've always been doing. You are correct, your borders are open. Some of your politicians and popular press talk of trying to close them again, but you touch eight other countries by land alone."

"Do not be forgetting the English and their Chunnel."

"Nine then, plus sea or air. Your borders are past closing. Your nation and others are still grounded in symmetric thinking in an asymmetric world. Don't waste time or effort on borders, instead spend all of your energies directly on the problem. To move the President, we don't lock down a city, instead we secure a path. Sorry I can't be more specific, ma'am. As I said, I'm just a sniper."

"And yet you know our borders enough to remember even Andorra, Monaco, and Luxembourg." The ambassador watched him for a long time, long enough for Roy to shuffle his feet. Sienna could see him preparing to apologize when the ambassador turned back to Sienna. She rested a warm hand on Sienna's arm and squeezed it gently.

"You must come to talk to our people. And you must bring this one with you. Oh, to be young in Paris once again." She squeezed Sienna's arm again with a totally different meaning, the first of confidence, then second in a woman-to-woman intimacy that Sienna had little experience with. Then Magda was gone.

"Wait!" But it was too late. "I don't have time to go to France," she told Roy for lack of anyone else to address.

Before he could respond, Frank Adams stepped up to them.

"Agent Beaumont. My office. Eight a.m. tomorrow."

"Yes, sir. May I ask why?"

"The President tells me the NSA is going to France."

Roy didn't even show surprise.

Sienna considered and decided that she wasn't surprised either. Magda Armand was not the French Ambassador by chance and must have already spoken with the President. And apparently, what the President knew, Frank Adams knew as well.

"Which means what to me?" Roy clenched his elbow against his side, as if to squeeze her fingers for reassurance.

She'd only be gone for a few days, far more than she could afford, but she'd be back.

Then Frank's smile turned positively evil as he faced Roy, perhaps finally finding a target for retribution after the forced revelation of his own story.

"Which means you're going to need to own more than one suit."

Chapter 5

Their walk back to Sienna's office passed in silence. Roy was puzzling at Frank's comment, but becoming no smarter for all his thinking. Maybe Dilya had somehow found out he only owned the one suit and told Adams. But what did it mean? Needing a second suit meant he'd be off the roof more. The White House roof was one of the few places in all of D.C., as far as he could tell, where a man could feel the wind and weather and have some degree of privacy.

It wasn't until they reached Sienna's office that his thoughts turned back to the present.

He leaned against the door jamb and watched her transformation. As she crossed the threshold her entire demeanor changed. She shifted like a sniper blending into the landscape. In the Residence she had been elegant and patient, thoughtful and unconsciously feminine. No hair flips, hip-swinging sashays, or any of the other wiles he typically observed; instead she was simply a beautiful woman operating in an arena dominated by men.

In her office she accelerated until she was almost a blur like The Flash: checking phone messages, tapping the space bar for a quick glance at the computer screen—followed by a grimace, probably at the number of new messages as she didn't pause to actually read any of them.

In seconds she'd also fetched her coat and changed from heels, that had done some wonderful things to the shape of her calves, into sneakers. It was another thing to like about her. She didn't retain the heels or change into designer flats. She now wore a tired pair of black converse with a complex white design drawn all over them. They were wholly inappropriate with the fancy dress and somehow wholly appropriate on Sienna Arnson.

With a startling efficiency, she was soon standing just a step away looking up at him. Looking farther up than he'd grown used to through the evening. Heeled, her five-six had became five-eight. Flat-footed she was made more female. He'd dated women both tall and short, but Sienna kept changing on him.

And still she merely watched him.

"What?"

"You're blocking the door," yet she was making no effort to get by him.

He was. "I am. Must say you have a comfortable door frame."

She rolled her eyes at him, but it earned him the laugh he'd been after. Her humor, like everything else, came from all of the way inside. Every one of her emotions was so clear and pure.

"How did you ever survive what you've been through and still be who you are?"

"Who *I* am?" As if she didn't understand the question. She wasn't playing coy, she really didn't know what she'd been doing to him all evening.

Of its own volition, one of his hands reached out to brush down her hair. Between one breath and the next, the NSA was again gone, and Sienna leaned her cheek into his palm.

He could find no words to express what she was doing to him.

Unable to resist her, he used that light pressure of cheek to palm to draw her toward him. She could have slipped away by merely straightening her head, but she eased forward as effortlessly and gracefully as any doe walking through the woods.

He didn't kiss her first. Or hold her first. Or…they simply came together in a single, body-long sensation from thighs to hands to lips.

Their first kiss had been a surprising accident of a whirlwind of emotions. Their second was of shared wonder. Roy had never been so aware of so many things at once. Her scent really was honey sweet, like the taste of a distant hive on a summer breeze, full of flowers and life. Her kiss was rich with depth. And her body—he was a goner. Her waist fit his hands as if custom formed for the purpose. When he dared to slide them down the least little bit, the rising curve of her hips brushed the inside of his palms.

She groaned as he pulled her in tighter, a ripple felt as much chest to chest as mouth to mouth. He couldn't get enough of her. Couldn't get her close enough. Had to—

"Whoa!" Sienna's protest came out on a half moan.

He pulled her in tighter and she gave against him for a long moment, before pulling back.

"Seriously, Roy. Whoa."

How was he supposed to stop when—

But the lady said stop. Unable to actually let go, he simply held her against him and nestled his face in her hair.

Her arms didn't withdraw from around his neck, she too continued to hold him as tightly as he did her.

Even in the heat of sex he'd never felt a woman the way he felt Sienna against him though they were both still fully clothed.

They remained unmoving for an impossibly long moment—one that he never wanted to end.

Then she eased a step back out of his arms and he, god help him, let her go. A gap of air formed between them, their final contact was his palm against her cheek that she trapped momentarily against her shoulder before he let his hand drop.

"Whoa!" She repeated one more time, though he'd already stopped.

#

"Whoa!" Sienna really needed to stop saying that. Her nerve endings were very, very happy, but her nerves had neared panic mode.

As her mental faculties slowly reengaged, she became aware again of their surroundings.

"This is my office."

Roy grunted an agreement sort of sound.

"We nearly did…something in my office."

Again the grunt of agreement.

She looked up at Roy and squinted her eyes at him trying to see the truth of his next answer. "This wasn't some male marking the female's territory was it?"

"I'm not a golden retriever."

"No," she had to agree with that. "More like a German shepherd, warm and cuddly but incredibly dangerous when aroused."

His smile told her that hadn't come out right.

"Maybe 'riled' would have been a better choice of words."

"Well, I admit that you're an arousing kind of lady. But I don't get riled up much." His gaze drifted up over her head and scanned the room. "As to pissing on your personal fire hydrant, can't say as it ever crossed my mind. Frankly your office scares the hell out of me, my Lady Sienna Aphrodite. Every time you stand here, I remember just what the hell you do for a living."

She turned and tried to see it through his eyes. It was one of the three largest private offices in the West Wing, other than the Oval of course. Right in a row along the west wall: the Chief of Staff, the Vice President, and the NSA. She had room for her disaster of a desk, a small circle of meeting chairs and a sofa by the window, and a table that could seat ten for a meal or a planning session. Every bit of furnishing and decoration was historic.

"Must say it scares the daylights out of me as well."

Roy slid his hands around her waist from behind.

It took only the slightest shift in weight to be leaning back against his chest.

"Somehow, Sienna, that doesn't make me feel much better. We snipers want our National Security Advisors to be supremely confident. You know, in addition to already being brilliant and stunningly beautiful."

"I'll file your request in a suggestion box. In the meantime I'll do my best to not show that I'm freaking out."

"Maybe this will help." He removed one hand from around her waist, and hit the light switch. The room was plunged into semi-darkness, only the lights of D.C. filtering through the sheer curtains she'd closed against an earlier sunset, and the open door behind them. Then he swung the door shut and he turned the lock with a click that seemed to echo through the room.

"What are you playing at, Roy?"

"Not playing, Sienna. 'Less you say stop, I mean to have my way with you."

The NSA was horrified at taking such a liberty in this pristine office. But he hadn't called her Ms. National Security Advisor. Not once in the whole evening, perhaps not once since she'd met him.

He always called her Sienna.

And it made all the difference in the world.

She was ready to be turned and pinned against the door. She was even ready to have her beautiful dress damaged as he tore it in a frantic need to get skin to skin. Neither thought upset her particularly.

What she wasn't ready for her was for him to wrap his arms back around her. He simply buried his face in her hair and held her tightly against him. She could feel his arousal pressing against her from behind, but he didn't make any moves.

Instead, he held her tighter and tighter until she could barely breathe. Then his hands began to roam. His rough calluses caught slightly on the jersey fabric and offered teasing glimpses of how his hands would feel on her skin.

"Having his way with her" was apparently a slow study. A hand brushing over the curve of her hip. The other sliding upward between her breasts, and a single finger tracing the line where her collarbone was revealed by the dress' scooped neckline. When his finger traced just the slightest rise of her revealed breasts, she wanted to shout at him to get on with it. But she discovered that this time she actually was far too close to hyperventilating to speak.

At quite which juncture his hands went from being outside the dress to the soft material being a puddle about her ankles and his hands on her skin, she couldn't quite trace back to the point of occurrence.

Though she absolutely remembered the moment he removed his own jacket and shirt. The flash of heat when he finally let them connect skin to skin took her knees right out from under her.

He let her momentum take them to the thick carpet.

"I don't—"

"I do," his whisper cut her off.

"You've had protection with you all night?" She actually giggled at the image of him shaking the President's hand with a pocketful of condoms. "At the reception?"

"Protection is part of my job." He actually said it with a matter-of-fact voice rather than a wry tone which had her giggle escalating.

"Did you bring more than one?"

"I didn't bring a whole box…but I came close. Do you always ask so many questions when a man is about to ravage you?"

Sienna figured she probably did. So she stopped and concentrated on giving as good as she received.

And Roy was absolutely incredible at making sure she truly received.

Chapter 6

Roy felt as if he'd slept a dozen hours, though he knew for a fact it was less than two. A man didn't get his chance with Sienna Arnson and waste a moment of it on sleep. Somewhere after they'd transitioned to his apartment, but before she'd demonstrated what she could do to him with a bar of soap in his shower, they had collapsed into his bed.

Not once had they performed the frantic-coupling-and-done that defined so many of his experiences. Not that all of their lovemaking had been slow or gentle, but it had been very mutual.

He'd learned many things about Sienna. She liked to snuggle. Most women clung, Sienna snuggled. She was easily enough embarrassed to appear shy or inexperienced, but like she did everything else, she made love with a complete commitment to the task at hand. She gave of herself more than any woman he'd ever had.

And whether it was due to imagination or prior experience—which he promised himself he'd never ask—she was a very creative woman. A couple of things he asked her to remember just what she'd done, because he'd been in such throes that his memory was faulty.

Like the shape and feel of her. She wasn't a workout queen, but he could feel the contours of the muscles that lay beneath that ever-so perfect skin. She must rule a stair stepper or some similar machine. Her glutes, when he cupped her exquisite behind with both hands to drag her more tightly against him, were astonishing.

So, he was on the bounce when he entered Frank Adams' cubbyhole office at one minute to eight the next morning.

And one look at Frank Adams' desk was enough to make him feel as if he hadn't slept in a week. Adams was one of those neat-freak managers, so his desk rarely held more than the day's duty roster and the all-important Action Sheet that was every known movement of all of the White House protectees. On the wall hung only two small photos: his and Beat's wedding photo and an autographed picture of the President shaking Frank's hand.

This morning there was a stack of four two-inch black training binders and Roy had the nasty feeling all of that reading was for him.

"Good morning, sir." He tried to make it as cheerful as he'd felt the moment before he stepped into the room, but Adams was back to being the Head of the PPD—one hundred percent hard-ass.

"Roy Beaumont," Frank flipped open a file, but didn't bother to look at it.

Roy could see it was his personnel file.

"You master every task I assign you more rapidly than any other man on my team, yet you make no effort of your own to improve your position."

"Kee Stevenson may have pointed that out to me earlier this week, sir." He'd meant to give it more thought, but spare time had been a little sparse on the ground these last few days.

"Sit, but don't speak again."

Roy sat and barely managed to bite back the "Yes, sir."

"You are one of the best technical shooters we have. Your teams consistently have better attention to task, even when you are merely a team member rather than a leader. The thorough analyses you made of route protection plans last week were both insightful and better than the double-blind originating marksman."

The first Roy had heard of it.

"And Ms. Stevenson remarked on your exceptional ability to acquire and integrate new skills rapidly." Adams closed the personnel file, still without looking down at it.

Then he slid the stack of training notebooks across the table. "You have forty-eight hours to digest these."

Roy had worked through these types of manuals before; it was technically possible to plow through one of them in a week if he did nothing else.

"Four—"

"I did not give you permission to speak yet, Beaumont."

Roy bit hard on his tongue, but kept his anger to himself.

Adams spun the pile so that Roy could see the bindings.

Head of Protection Detail Procedures

Protection Detail Management: Domestic

Protection Detail Management: Abroad, France

National Security Advisor: Protection Requirements and Methodology

Adams was turning him into the head of Sienna's Protection Detail.

"Now you can speak."

Roy didn't know what he'd say if he could. But it didn't matter, he couldn't manage a word.

"Yeah, bro," Frank's voice slid into a funky uptown Manhattan, way uptown, that Roy had never heard from him. "Dat exactly how I be feelin' when dis shit come down on top o' *my* head." It was a level of accent that couldn't be faked. Frank Adams was from the streets of upper Manhattan, maybe even the projects by the sound of it, and that was a bad place to climb out of. What's more, he was revealing his past to Roy who had never even heard it whispered about.

"But I'll be responsible for…" Roy gestured helplessly toward Sienna's office, "…her life."

Frank dropped his accent and said kindly, "Welcome to the club, Beaumont. Now get to work."

Roy took his manuals and got.

# # #

Sienna tried not to be piqued when Roy didn't respond to her message asking if he could join her for a quick lunch.

It was harder when he ignored the dinner request.

If this was his idea of morning-after treatment she was going to murder him. The man didn't get to wholly redefine "great sex"—which he absolutely had—and also lead her to discover an inner passion that she hadn't known she possessed, and then get all…*guy* on her.

Knowing that Roy's life wasn't necessarily in his control, she tried to take it easy, but every time she looked about her office, she couldn't.

She believed that he had no intention of "marking" her territory, yet he absolutely had.

This morning she'd taken two steps through the door and been standing on exactly the first place they had made love. It would always be that spot of carpet, right there by the door, their first time ever together. And the couch he'd eased her onto afterward and given her a splendid naked massage while his body had recovered enough for her to take him by straddling his lap while he sat in the chair she usually occupied at the head of the conference table. They'd flirted and petted against the side of her desk when she had to turn on the desk lamp to locate her underwear, which for reasons unknown had been in the exact middle of the conference table.

It was by the soft glow of that lamp that they had stood back and inspected each other. Roy's sturdy power wasn't only in his face and his strength went far beyond his hands. He was beautiful in the way a Navy destroyer was—his looks so perfectly suited to what he was: incredibly male. And his long soft whistle as he inspected her had left her blushing and foolishly pleased. It wasn't a wolf whistle, but rather one of simple astonishment. And all of that had been only a prelude to the romp at his apartment. Completely unlike her, wholly unbelievable, and absolutely glorious.

Then today Roy Beaumont had gone silent though they worked only one floor apart in the same building.

She didn't have time for dinner anyway, so by nine o'clock she was exhausted, hungry, and the woman in her needed some slight reassurance that the best night of her sexual life had *not* been a one-night stand. She dropped down the stairs by the Cabinet Room that landed close by the door into the Secret Service ready room. If Roy wasn't there, maybe she could still find Frank Adams.

She spotted Roy right away, it wasn't difficult as he was the only person in the land of low cubicles and conference tables. He was at the far back of the room studying something on his desk.

"Hey there."

He didn't respond.

She wove her way in between the tables. One had maps of Boston and a binder labeled "Presidential travel: July 12." A whole set of tables had an Africa tour laid out on them country by country even though she knew that wasn't scheduled until September.

She tried another "Hey!" when she was nearly to Roy.

Nothing.

That's when she realized he was asleep sitting up. His head was propped up on his fist. A black notebook was opened before him. She read the page title: *Acceptable vehicle selection for protectee* transport post-attack (categorized by medical condition). A list of vehicles followed with advantages and disadvantages listed.

No wonder the man was asleep.

His desk included the remains of a couple of sandwiches. There were also several cans of Coke. If she drank that many in a day she'd be vibrating with manic energy for a week, yet Roy slept. His phone lay on the desk, shoved to the side. She tapped it awake and could see her text messages.

When she touched his shoulder, he jolted awake as fast as his phone screen. It wasn't some smooth, clean rousing of a lover. One moment Roy was completely out, the next moment he had a hand clamped around her wrist and his other hand resting on the butt of his sidearm.

"Oh. Sorry." He let her go immediately and looked at her with those clear blue eyes that were wide awake. They were the eyes of a wide awake *agent* triggered into full alert mode.

She waited as his gaze slowly softened. When he finally smiled, she figured the *man* was now awake as well.

"Hey beautiful," he murmured after glancing about the room to make sure they were alone. Definitely awake.

"Hey yourself. You didn't answer my messages."

He scrabbled for his phone, checked them, and cursed. "Sorry, I set the damn thing on silent so that I could concentrate."

"Yeah, I see you concentrating," she made a deeply nasal snoring sound.

"Didn't realize I'd nodded off. It's a bit dry," he slapped at the notebook in disgust.

"What are you reading?" She flipped it closed to read the title.

He grabbed it to block her, but the open notebook had been propped against three others.

Her attention jumped straight to: *National Security Advisor: Protection Requirements and Methodology* then *Head of Protection Detail Procedures.*

"Adams made you…" she couldn't even say it. She could process information quickly, but this was too much. Too big.

"The head of your protection detail? Yes. At least through France."

"You would…" How in the hell was it possible? "Take a bullet for me?"

"Lady," he reached out and took her chilled hand in his big, warm one. "I'd have done that since the first time I met you."

It was too big for Sienna to comprehend. But she did know one thing for certain, there was going to be at least one more morning-after.

She tugged on their joined hands.

"Lady, I need my sleep tonight."

"So do I," she agreed and managed to get him moving. "So we won't try to finish the rest of your protection supply just tonight…maybe only half of it."

They barely managed to use one before passing out in each others' arms.

Chapter 7

It was Adams himself who drilled Roy the morning before the flight.

And Roy totally blew it. He had the reporting structure correct, but the timing of "all safe" updates wrong. He kept allotting more duties to himself than he should have as head of detail.

"Trust your people to do their part of the job," Adams admonished him again and again. Then completely destroyed the lesson by saying, "But if anything goes wrong it lands a hundred percent on you, not on them."

Adams kept at him for two hours and Roy would swear that half of it wasn't anywhere in the manuals. Throughout the interview Adams didn't refer to the manuals or any testing sheet. Everything must be engraved in his memory. That's when Roy realized that a lot of those procedures had probably been written or at least heavily updated by Adams personally. It made him both more and less daunting. Those books represented every practical lesson learned by prior protection details since the

1901 assassination of President McKinley. Adams had had to flog his way through them once upon a time and then enhance them from his own experience.

The idea that Roy might be adding to those one day wandered into his sights and he liked the way that thought felt. He would have to study them more on the flight.

Adams slipped a plastic-coated card across his desk to Roy. Rather than being some sort of a failing grade, it was a list of contacts. Secret Service overseas, USEUCOM search and rescue, French Ministry of Defence, the French COS (their version of the US Special Operational Command), Paris police… It was an amazing compendium of phone numbers and radio frequencies.

"Now forget the damn manuals," Adams waved a dismissive hand. "Trust your instincts. We've spent a lot of money training those over the years. Remember! Nothing is more important than the survival of your protectee, nothing. You come under friendly fire from a Paris SWAT team, you find a way to take out that SWAT team and clean up the political fallout later. If there's a bomb blast, there had better be a Beaumont-shaped shadow covering your protectee. We clear?"

"Clear, sir." Despite his desperate need for sleep, he'd lain awake for hours the last two nights with Sienna snuggled hard against him. Whether it was his Yankee upbringing, his father's taciturn training, or something inside himself, he'd always felt the need to protect. The Secret Service had been a clean fit to his way of thinking.

But with Sienna curled back against him, his arm tucked around her, and her fingers laced into his even in sleep, he'd found an entirely new meaning to the need to protect. He'd been trained endlessly that his life was less important than that of the person he was protecting until it came to him naturally. He'd thankfully never had that training tested in a real-life situation, but he didn't anticipate any of the common problems like freezing under fire or second thoughts.

He hadn't been exaggerating when he'd told Sienna he'd have taken a bullet for her from the first time they'd met. There was something precious about her. The world would be a lesser place without her in it. And his own world was infinitely expanded by having her in it. He'd finally slept with his nose in her hair and woken with her in his arms. Nothing was more important than preserving that.

"Roy," Adams eased back in his chair and sounded almost friendly, the way a black bear appeared friendly the moment before it tore you into tiny pieces. "Your instincts are among the best I've ever seen. Trust them. Because, believe me, nothing prepares you for when it goes wrong. If it makes you feel any better, when it does go south and you feel like you're just making it up as you go, we've all done the same."

"You?"

"There was a carefully underreported incident where it came down to Beat and I, the President and the future First Lady under heavy fire in a foreign country. You'll be too busy to be terrified or worry; that's when your instincts will kick into gear." Then he offered a wry smile, "The shakes will come later though, that I can promise." Then he straightened up. "Now get the hell out of my office. I've got work to do."

Roy stood at his own desk out in the main area and decided Adams was right, to hell with the books. Now it was time to start thinking about his own detail.

He considered for a long minute, then messaged the Paris office. He'd pick up two stringers and a pair of vehicles from the office there for his team. Then he prepped a pair of flight cases. In the first one he packed his sidearm, his backup, and a Glock 43 for Sienna if there was an emergency. He signed out five extra magazines for each, because if that didn't do it, they'd be done for anyway.

In the second case he put the new CSASS rifle. It wasn't even in distribution yet, but he'd been part of the team to test the Compact Semi-Automatic Sniper System and he completely agreed with the selection of Heckler & Kock's modified G28 as the new weapon of choice. And at the moment he appreciated it all the more because it folded down neatly to two-and-a-half feet long rather than the typical four to five feet for a top sniper rifle. He made sure that he had the clearance paperwork for all four weapons. He almost tossed in the *National Security Advisor: Protection Requirements and Methodology* manual as well, but decided that Adams probably knew what he was talking about.

Then he laughed. Of course Adams knew. He'd asked Roy plenty of questions this morning that weren't in the manuals. As much as he'd been testing Roy, he'd also been teaching, making sure Roy knew what he needed most. He dumped the damn manual back on the desk, tapped the laminated contacts card tucked in his shirt pocket, and strode out of the office, giving Adams a cocky wave.

Then he'd slunk back in for his own suitcase and jacket.

# # #

"I'm sorry, Roy," Sienna greeted him as soon as they met out at Andrews Field. She lugged one of those square black cases that lawyers and airline pilots always carried. He took it from her and almost dropped it.

"Thing weighs a ton."

"All of the prep materials I need for France but haven't had time to look at. I'm going to have to work the whole flight. I'd sort of hoped—"

"Not much privacy," he pointed at the plane waiting for them on the tarmac. The National Security Advisor was rated as a mid-level protectee. The high-levels included: the First and Second Families, Presidential candidates who'd won a few primaries, visiting world leaders, and occasional high-risk individuals.

Mid-levels like the White House Chief of Staff, the NSA, and the majority and minority leaders of the Congress almost always had an agent driver and someone watching their home.

Roy had been aware of the agent who had discreetly followed them back to his house the three nights that he and Sienna had managed together. If Sienna had noticed, she gave no sign.

Low-levels were on the lists and watched, but not constantly monitored. Dilya was a low-level when she was at school, but a high-level when she was traveling with the First Daughter.

When a mid-level picked up an overseas assignment, their team size increased two-to ten-fold depending on a wide variety of factors. One thing it earned them was a private jet. In the NSA's case, it was a ten-seater Gulfstream G450—a small, sleek aircraft that would punch across the Atlantic in just six hours.

But a G450 offered no privacy for what he wouldn't have minded spending the ocean crossing concentrating on.

"I," Sienna sounded a bit indignant, "do not have a one-track gutter mind."

"But you make it such a nice one-track gutter to contemplate."

"Hey."

"What?"

"Look at me."

He hadn't realized that he wasn't. He'd been busy inspecting the security. Outer layer guards. An immaculate cleanliness to the hangar and the base that made it much harder to hide things that didn't belong. The behemoths of this part of the airfield, the four jets of the Air Force One and Air Force Two fleet had a standing honor guard. The Gulfstream 450 presently boasted a guard herself in addition to two pilots and a mechanic going over their preflight checks.

"Sorry. Habit. I'm just checking security."

"Now I'm the one who is sorry. Go back to doing that."

"But pay attention to you while I'm doing it?"

"Of course."

"The problem with looking at you, Goddess Sienna Aphrodite, it makes it hard for me to concentrate on anything else." He offered her a leer which earned him a laugh, then he turned to inspect where he would set up if he was a sniper aiming at the

NSA or her plane. He was pleased to see that the most likely hides were all inside the base's security perimeter.

"What I was saying before some rude, crude gentleman interrupted me—"

"Never have been accused of being a gentleman before." They headed across the tarmac between the hangar and the airplane which opened up new ranges of fire that were *not* inside the Joint Base Andrews' perimeter. A peek-a-boo view of a low office building to the east would be his first choice. Even though it would be a lousy and difficult shot, he slowed a half step to keep between it and Sienna.

"I had been hoping that we could talk a bit during the flight, as I was *fully aware* that we wouldn't have the privacy for what I really want to do. See, women sometimes have one-track minds as well."

"I admit to liking the one-track. The talking I'm less sure about."

She was quiet as they handed off the luggage to the pilot. He handed the paperwork for the two weapons cases to him as well. The pilot read them very carefully, inspected the contents, countersigned that he was aware they were aboard, and stowed them with the baggage. Roy went aboard carrying only a small notebook, his phone, and Sienna's massive briefcase.

They settled in their seats.

"Soda, beer, and wine in the fridge at the rear," the copilot pointed as he boarded. "Some snacks too. This morning's inflight movie is Tom Hanks in *Castaway* and then—"

"Then," the pilot came up behind him, "Your choice of Harrison Ford crashing into the ocean in *Air Force One* or *White House Down*. Yeah, yeah." He nudged the copilot forward. "You folks need anything, just let us know, otherwise you can self-serve." He closed and latched the outside door, then entered the cockpit himself, sliding a privacy curtain half closed. A clear message of: 'We'll leave you alone, but you're welcome to duck your head in.'

"So, you're not much of a one for talking?" Sienna teased him.

Not one for talking? He'd talked more to her than all of the rest of the women in his life…combined. And she made it so damn fun. She didn't judge him for having less education or worldly experience. Instead she listened to what he said, gave him the space to develop his thoughts.

It had been a joy to offer her the same. Sienna's conversations ranged far and wide. She joined together scattered bits and pieces into logical, sensible structures. Then she turned around and tried to tear them back apart. It had become one of his favorite games with her, watching her build those clear towers of thought and then help her poke holes and dig out crevices while she struggled to patch them back together with new ideas.

"Nope," he teased back. "Never was much of a talker."

"Liar."

"Well, not before you. You make me feel…" He wasn't sure how to finish that sentence and thankfully the plane's engines winding to life gave him an excuse to leave off.

Sienna Arnson made him feel so…alive. As if he'd been asleep on his feet for years and was finally coming awake.

He looked across the table at her. They'd sat in a pair of comfortable seats that had more in common with armchairs than his usual coach-class airplane seats. He'd taken a backward facing seat, letting her fly forward. There was a matching setup across the aisle and a sofa to the stern, facing across the cabin to a large-screen television.

Her attention was already drifting down into the first of the thick briefing folders she'd extracted from the case by her feet. Any strands of hair that had slipped loose from the roll at the back of her head, she slipped between her lips. She didn't chew on it, but simply trapped it between clamped lips as she concentrated.

They taxied away from the hangar and the pilot announced they were first in line for takeoff so they should "hang onto their stirrups."

He'd come to know every curve of her features, even how they changed, like the shape of her cheek when she smiled. The angle of her shoulders when she was exhausted or fresh off a workout. The way her eyes narrowed when she was concentrating, yet her brow remained clear and unfurrowed. He wondered how time would change her. He was a little surprised to realize that he'd like to be around to find out. It was easier to imagine waking beside her every day than not doing so.

Every day for how long, Beaumont?

He wasn't used to such a question. Thinking about his future hadn't preoccupied him much over the years, as both Kee and Adams had pointed out. They were smart people who he respected immensely, so maybe it was time he started.

The engines roared to life and the plane bolted down the runway.

So: *every day for how long, Beaumont?*

He couldn't imagine ever not wanting to be beside her when she woke.

He could imagine her with…

"Do you want children?"

"Do I what?" Sienna shouted back over the takeoff roar, but her look of shock showed that hearing him wasn't the problem. The folder she'd opened fell to the floor and she didn't even notice.

Now that he'd asked the question, he did want to know the answer. He shrugged, at something of a loss to identify where the question came from. Partly Frank and Beat's choice, partly the mischievous Dilya, and partly the gorgeous First Lady with the cutest kid ever.

The plane lifted and took to the sky.

Sienna watched him without speaking until they were well aloft.

"Do you?" She asked softly once the engine noise had dropped enough to speak normally.

He wanted to shrug, as if it wasn't any real difference to him one way or another. But the images from the White House reception were too clear. He'd never really thought about kids, no more than he'd thought about his long-term career. He was a shooter, that's what he did—until he suddenly became the head of the NSA's protection detail.

Kids were part of being a normal family, at least for others—until he imagined Sienna's children. He could see her with them so easily.

But not if they were another man's.

"Yes," he finally answered. "Yes, I do want kids. If they're with you."

# # #

That shot went straight to Sienna's heart, slamming her back into the plane seat. She tried to see into Roy and discover where the question had come from.

Well, parts of that were easy. Frank, Beat, Dilya, the First Kid: they all added up to make a man think about children.

But that wasn't what he'd said.

He'd said, *If they're with you.*

She wanted to parse and analyze the words. Break them down for inner meaning and nuance.

But Roy was too forthright a speaker. When he meant something, he said it in as many words. Any other man, any decent man who wasn't trying to make her crazy, would have said, "I don't know where that question came from. But I'm just kinda curious if you were one of those women who wanted a family or are you some kind of careerist?" Complete with insulting tone as if the two were so mutually exclusive.

And Roy had said, *If they're with you.*

"But we've only known each other for—" She had no idea. She knew him so well, but did she know him at all?

"Seven days as of 10:17 a.m. tomorrow morning. That's East Coast time. 15:17 Paris time."

"Seven days?"

"Six days and eleven minutes as of right now," he tipped his watch in her direction as if to prove his point.

"Six days and eleven minutes?" She wasn't making any headway with the concept. She'd once lived with a man for six months, even been talking about becoming engaged, and didn't begin to know him as well as she knew Roy.

"Twelve now," he smiled. "Not that I'm counting."

"And you want to know if I want to have children?"

"Uh-huh."

"With you?"

"Uh-huh."

"Did you just propose to me?" Even if he didn't connect the two, Sienna knew that he wasn't the sort of man to talk about having children out of wedlock.

Roy blinked hard. But he didn't have the decency to look abashed for more than a few moments. "Huh."

"Huh?" It had been a very noncommittal sound.

"Can't say as that's what I was asking. Six days and twelve minutes seems a might bit quick for that."

"Thank god."

"So let's table that part of it."

Sienna sagged, but it wasn't only with relief. She had to admit that there was just a little disappointment there as well which, as Roy might say, was surprising as all hell.

"For now, anyway," as if he was reading her thoughts. "But I would like to know your answer to the first question."

"Children? With you?"

"Just askin'."

Never having had a conversation like this one (Ever! Anywhere!), Sienna didn't have much to go on.

There would be no synthesizing a well-researched set of options into an actionable scenario. There was no National Security Advisor report or think-tank modeling she could fall back on.

Children? With Roy?

The second part was easier to answer. She'd seen him with the children at the museum. And she'd listened to the lessons of the forest taught by his reticent father, but inhaled by the child right down to his core. Even his treating Dilya as an intelligent grownup rather than dismissing her as some teenaged girl.

With Roy? No question. It was hard to imagine a man who'd be a better father.

Actual children? Little Siennas running about the house? That was far trickier.

She watched out the window as shore gave way to bay, then after a brief splash of green that was Delaware, true ocean. To hold a child who reached up and mussed her hair at a glittering party. To watch her turn into whatever version of Dilya the girl might become. Or a boy cut from the same cloth as Roy Beaumont. There was a truly breathtaking image.

She looked back at him, waiting patiently. All of his attention focused on her as he waited for her answer. A man who thought her answers were as important as his own. Who had proved time and again that he thought her pleasure was as essential as his own. A man of such integrity that he wouldn't even steal a kiss when it was offered because of some whimsical challenge.

"Yes," the word slipped out on its own, but she felt no desire to take it back. Children with Roy only had one answer, though she repeated it just to try its flavor, "With you? Yes."

He nodded carefully, "Good to know." Then his smile lit up and erased any doubt she might have.

The insanity of the moment set her to giggling. She wasn't ready to marry Roy but would have his children without a moment's further doubt. It was too crazy. Her giggle escalated, she couldn't tamp it back down.

Roy finally caught the ludicrous edge of the situation and added his own low laugh to hers.

"Just be damned glad there's no privacy, Roy Beaumont. Or I might let you start trying right on that couch back there."

He glanced over his shoulder at the half-closed curtain, then back at her with an eager grin she'd long since learned to recognize.

"No, Beaumont. Just…no!"

"Spoilsport," he muttered though she could tell he wasn't really serious.

An eager grin she'd long since learned to recognize.
Long since.

Six days and twenty-whatever minutes ago he'd been a total stranger. They had been together for a grand total of three nights. But it didn't feel like infatuation. It felt like nothing that had come before. There was no thought necessary to know how she felt.

It was a damn good thing he'd taken back his second, unintended question.

For now, he'd said. Not really taking it away.

Three nights together that felt like three months they were so familiar and comfortable. Always at his place for obvious reasons. Her abrupt return to Washington, D.C. at the President's request had caught her unprepared. Since stepping in as the new NSA, she was living in her parents' home this past week. She'd meant to find a place of her own, but hadn't had a moment to think about that yet.

She retrieved the folder that had slipped out of her fingers at Roy's question and opened it on the table between them. Then she leaned forward.

"Roy?"

"Uh-huh."

"When we get back…"

"Yes?"

"Let's have dinner and stay at my place."

"Sure thing."

He knew where she was living, but he wasn't making the connection quite yet.

"I think it's time I brought my boyfriend home to share a meal with my parents."

"Uh—Uuuh!" The wind came out of him as if he'd just been punched in the gut.

Which seemed only fair after what he'd done to her. Now Paris was approaching far too quickly, so she turned back to her work.

She was pleased to notice that it took Roy a fair amount of time before he started breathing normally again.

Chapter 8

*R*oy *looked out the* window at the hangar and grimaced.

He'd specifically set up their landing at a remote hangar at Paris-Orly. It was supposed to have a grand total of two agents and two unremarkable cars.

"Wow!" Sienna was looking at him. "Who just got on your bad side? I'm guessing their life expectancy has plummeted in the last five seconds."

"Good guess," he gestured out the window and she looked. A line of five black Citroën DS5 sedans were waiting for them, looking like a school of sleek racing machines ready to eat alive anyone who got in their way. A cloud of motorcycle police were waiting as well.

By the time the plane halted, he wouldn't have been surprised if a marching band trooped in. At least there weren't any reporters.

"Stay!" He pointed to Sienna in her seat and clambered out of the plane as soon as the steps were down. A line of very formally dressed Frenchmen and women organized themselves by the cars.

"This is for me?" Of course Sienna hadn't stayed put. They were going to have to talk about that.

"No. It's for some other National Security Advisor."

"Oh. Right. New to the job, I keep forgetting. I guess this is my show. So, *you* stay." She made it funny, then trooped forward with her two-ton briefcase in tow.

A man dressed in recognizable protection department suit came up and handed over his ID. "Jankowski. This is Chen." Per standard, because they were overseas, the two were Diplomatic Security Service people—close enough to being the foreign version of the Secret Service to work just fine.

Kristian Jankowski, the DSS three-year man was a sturdy Pole, just like his name, with a Brooklyn accent mostly erased. Sandy blond hair kept reasonably short.

Mabel Chen, he'd stick with her last name, was a tiny Chinese woman who was too slender to be wearing a shoulder holster. But her small purse swung heavy so he'd trust to her six years in the DSS that she knew how to get to her weapon when necessary. He handed back their IDs.

"You two aren't exactly low profile."

"What did you expect?" Chen asked with a distinctly Midwestern accent, "a couple of suave Frenchmen in natty suits? This is Paris in the 21st century, we fit in just fine. At least I do. Jankowski has a wife; she's like some crazy mix Italian-Jewish-mother from Scotland. It makes him certifiable. Which now that I've said it, makes him fit in just fine as well."

"And I'm loving it," Jankowski put in. "Gotta find a man for you, Chen."

"Like that'll solve my problems."

"Or a woman," Jankowski was perfectly amenable.

Chen ignored him. "How about you, Yankee Boy? You on the loose? What are you doing after we deliver your package to somewhere safe?"

Roy chose to follow Chen's lead and ignore her comment as the best course of action. But he liked the easy back and forth between her and Jankowski. It told him that they had been together a while and worked well as a team.

"Couldn't you have been even more visible?" He changed the subject.

"Sure," Chen nodded, her long dark ponytail fluttering in the light breeze. "We're in France. We could have hired some mimes or something. Why? You gonna be an asshole about it?"

"No," Roy looked down at her, way down. If she broke five feet it would be a miracle. "I'm gonna be an asshole about this goddamn parade instead of my requested two vehicles."

Sienna was busy doing a glad hand with all sorts: some in military uniforms, others in a slightly more elegant version of Washington-dulls to mark them as governmental uniforms.

Chen pointed. Behind the cavalcade sat a pair of sedans: a newish blue BMW X5 SUV and an older gray Mercedes C-Class that no one would ever mistake for an executive vehicle. About as nondescript as a man could desire.

"Shit!"

"Tell me about it," Chen groaned. "We had the site pretty well checked out—hangar secure, scouting the area—then *they* rolled in sirens and all."

"Okay, not your bad. Let me grab our bags. I have a couple cases Customs is going to take their time with."

"I got it for ya," Jankowski went and collected the bags that the pilot had unloaded.

"We sure aren't doing crap else with all this going on," Chen finished for him.

Normally Roy could fit a week of gear into a small knapsack. He hated that now he had suits, shirts, and dress shoes. At least Sienna traveled about as lightly as he did, except for the briefcase she had consumed during the flight. He had watched in fascination as she went through it all—literally all.

She made few notes, mostly she read, but then she'd suddenly jump back three folders and double-check some fact, often without having to hunt for it. Her memory must be photographic.

No, or she wouldn't have to look back. Pattern recognition. He'd wager that she remembered which folder, roughly where in the stack, and the general look of the page she wanted.

With different training, how good a sniper would she have been? Very, was his guess.

With different training could he be the NSA? There was a complete laugh.

He moved up to the group at the same moment that a customs officer put in an appearance.

"Passports please?" He asked in lightly accented English.

Once Sienna's had been barely glanced at and stamped, Roy handed over his along with his Secret Service ID, and the list of weapons and ammunition he was transporting into the country. The official glanced at the list, inspected Roy for a moment, then signed the customs release with a flourish and stamped his passport.

"I will ask that you try to refrain from shooting anyone while in France, the paperwork is enormous," he winked.

Roy winked back, though he didn't feel like it.

"We're in this car," Sienna sounded a little breathless from all of the attention.

"Hold on a moment." Roy doubled back to his DSS team. "What's your frequency?"

Chen told him.

He turned on his radio, set the frequency, and shoved in his earpiece. "Got me?"

"Five by five, Yankee Boy."

"Okay," he took the handgun case from Jankowski. He holstered his own Glock 21 at the shoulder, dropped his backup into his ankle holster, and slid the Glock 43 for Sienna into his back holster. He took two magazines for each and dropped them into his pockets.

"You expecting that kind of trouble?" Chen had sobered.

"Nope. Just like to be ready for it when it shows up." He also took the rifle broken down in its soft case so that it looked like little more than a tourist knapsack. He stuffed the other three magazines for each sidearm into the pack's side pockets and gave them back the empty handgun case. "Don't follow. Take some other route."

"Why?"

"I don't want our two vehicles identified with these," he waved at the line of black Citroëns. "But be close enough that I can call you."

They nodded and he went to sit beside Sienna in the deep leather of the Citroën DS5. The whole way into the center of the city with Sienna and whoever else it was in the car—he hadn't bothered to pay any attention to introductions yet—he felt like a bug on the road. Any moment a big-ass windshield could come along and they'd be flattened.

The police drove like maniacs, performing maneuvers he wouldn't have risked on a closed training circuit, never mind in Paris traffic. The steady, "Bee-boop! Bee-boop!" of their sirens was really getting on his nerves. When they roared up to the roundabout encircling the Arc de Triomphe they actually closed the busiest road he'd ever seen for the flashing instant it took the motorcade to surge through the intersection.

He kept his silence through security into the governmental center where they'd be holding the meetings.

They had a metal detector, but on flashing his Secret Service ID, he was waved through the detector which offered a shrill burp of complaint but was ignored.

He made it up to the fifth floor conference room. It had those crazy high French ceilings with curlicues and ornamentation that probably went back to some dead emperor. It would clearly be the working space for their meetings, but for now it was a reception complete with liveried waiters bearing trays of alcohol and hors d'oeuvres.

When one of the ministers asked him how the flight was, he couldn't hold it in any longer.

# # #

"What the hell is *wrong* with you people?"

Roy's shout almost made Sienna flip the flute of champagne she'd just been handed into the French President's face.

There was a sudden stunned silence.

Sienna had never seen Roy mad and it was a terrifying sight. He'd said that he didn't get riled much and she now knew that was a good thing. She wanted to cower, and his ire wasn't even aimed at her. He had grown until he was more imposing than Frank and Beatrice combined. How could she have considered life with this man when she didn't even know he was capable of such raw…fury.

It was clear by the pin-drop silence that everyone was as shocked as she was.

That meant that it was up to her to tame the unexpected beast in their midst.

She sidled up to his side, almost reached out, but on second thought pulled her hand back, remembering how hard he had grabbed her when roused from a sound sleep.

"Roy?" She tried to make her voice soft and soothing. Instead it acted like a trigger.

"You!" It was clear he was addressing the entire room and wasn't going to be soothed until he'd had his say.

Protocol would suggest a shrug of apology to the President, but Roy had never struck her as being irrational. She would give him the benefit of the doubt and just pray he didn't destroy US-French relations in the meantime.

"You ask the National Security Advisor to come to Paris because you are tired of being targets. Good! She's glad to help. France has been a good ally. Then you make that show at the airport—not to mention the drive here—as if to tell every single terrorist that an exceptionally high-value target has just arrived in Paris. A protection detail I could have been managed with three agents will now require twenty or more."

Sienna hadn't even thought of that. And he was absolutely right. His words to Madame Ambassador at the White House Residence had stuck with her as she'd reviewed all of the briefing reports on the flight over. They'd colored her thinking, forcing her to dig deeper…but not deep enough.

"Sir," Roy turned to General Dumont dressed in his full military dress uniform complete with gold braids dangling from shoulder to chest and the red band around his billed cap. "I'm sure that you, like the United States, train your soldiers not to salute when in the field because it draws a sniper's target on the officer's chest."

Dumont nodded carefully.

"So why did you draw one on the American National Security Advisor? If there had been a single photographer there, I would have put her on the plane and sent her right back home. We move the President in public because we have no other choice; his profile is too high. But with all of your pleasant show you are sending flyers to every terrorist: 'Here are my most valuable assets. Hit them, please.'"

Again the shocked silence,

Roy scrubbed at his face. "My apologies for the tone of my outburst," then he looked about the room before continuing more calmly. "But no apologies for my words. You have made my job here harder, that's fine. It's my job and I'll do it. You have endangered an honored guest. I'm sure that she was briefed on the dangers before she accepted the President's request to act as his NSA."

Sienna nodded confirmation. But all of the Secret Service's briefings on varying attack scenarios, including issuing her a pass to the White House bunker in case of attack—a particularly rare item—hadn't brought the message home as clearly as Roy's tirade.

"But I ask you to consider, is this clusterf— Is this *fiasco* typical in your protection plans for your own people and your own country? If they are, it's time to wake up and start thinking.

If you need another example: I'm a complete unknown to you. I stepped off a plane and waved a badge any decent forger could have made in a few hours."

Then he unholstered his sidearm and thumped it down on the fine wooden table, that probably dated back to the seventeenth century, hard enough to make everyone wince. Then he pulled a second one from his back waistband and thudded it down beside the other.

Five magazines followed, including one for his ankle piece though he didn't reach for that. He noticed the fifth magazine of .22s and slipped that one back into his pocket without comment. He didn't touch his knapsack that she hadn't seen him wearing before, which made her wonder what it contained.

"Enough rounds to shoot everyone in this room twice. Five of you would get shot three times if I don't miss. Any takers? You trusted me with no more reason than you wanted to believe that friends of your country were getting off an unmarked plane. This time you got lucky. Next time maybe you won't. Wake up people."

# # #

"Way to start my meeting off with a bang, Roy."

"Glad to help," he still sounded gruffly angry as he led her down a corridor she hadn't recalled traversing on the way to the conference room six hours earlier.

Their entire arrival had been overwhelming and elegantly French from the shining motorcade to the ornate décor including statues, murals, and paintings they'd passed enroute to this room. It had been thrilling…until Roy unloaded both verbal barrels on them.

The reception had collapsed before it started. When talk resumed, it was already focused on the topic of her visit. Soon they had cleared the waiters out of the room and were discussing existing security strategies over empty champagne glasses and trays of abandoned canapés.

Now, Roy was leading her into some nether region of the building that still had carpeting, but it was thin and there was little else going for the decorations.

"Where are we going?"

"Not where they expect," and she heard the smile in his voice.

"Which is?"

"There are a dozen agents waiting in the garage: four vehicles, black Ford Explorers with tinted glass, very hard to miss."

"But you said—"

"There is a police escort up on the street waiting to guide them to your hotel room at the Hotel Raphael Paris." He yanked open a door, cursed soundly at the occupant when he discovered it was an office. Sienna only had a moment to see her wide-eyed alarm before Roy slammed the door shut again.

She pointed to the next door down the hall clearly marked *Sortie*.

"But—"

"Where, my apologies to both you and the Raphael, you won't be staying." He entered the stairwell as if it was a room-clearing target rather than deep inside a highly secure governmental center.

"I won't?" She had to scramble to keep up with him as he descended the five flights of steel stairs. At a small door, a lone security guard sat at a metal detector waiting for anyone to actually use this entrance at eight at night. He looked bored to death with his obscure outpost in the labyrinthine building.

Roy merely waved at him as they exited without even turning so that his face would be seen. It seemed rude, but she did the same. Two people exit quietly. Wholly unmemorable.

"You won't. The caravan will arrive at the hotel and I wish I could see how long it takes whoever is watching to determine that no one is getting out except for Service agents."

There were two cars parked at the curb—neither one a black-and-tinted SUV. Roy escorted her into the backseat of the first one then slid in beside her.

"Beaumont! Where are you taking me?"

"Mabel here," he hooked a thumb toward the Chinese driver who couldn't possibly be named that, but kept his attention outside the car, "highly recommends a small hotel in the fifth district."

Sienna turned to look at the second car. It was following them, but not too closely.

"No," Roy admonished her. "Don't do that. It draws attention to the other vehicle."

"Oh? And you trying to look out every window at once isn't just as obvious?"

"She's got you there, Yankee Boy," the driver said in alarmingly familiar American. Perhaps she *could* be named Mabel.

Roy leaned back with a sigh. His only other concession to her being right was a soft curse of, "Crap!"

Chapter 9

*R*oy, *Sienna decided, was* a very tricky man.

She'd been afraid that after his tirade he was going to turn her into some kind of prisoner. She'd never been to Paris with a beau and had looked forward to seeing some of the world's most romantic city together.

But he didn't lock her up. Quite the opposite.

"They're expecting a redheaded beauty with a phalanx of guards hitting the high end of Paris' offerings. So put on a blouse and nice slacks then tuck your pretty hair under a scarf. The four of us are going out to dinner as two cheerful couples."

And they had. Sienna would bet that her dinner in a classic French street-café with three Secret Service agents had been far more enjoyable than a meal with the ministers she'd spent the afternoon and evening with. The only oddity to the meal had been when Roy seated her, he set her with her back to the Place de la Sorbonne where the sidewalk café was half tucked under the trees and his own back to a wall.

"Wouldn't I be safer if it was my back to the wall?"

He'd eyed her in a way that said she just might end up that way later—they did have connecting rooms. "Field of view. Yes, your back is to most of the crowds. However, that means I have a broad view of anyone who may be coming at you. Chen is watching east and Jankowski west. We've got you covered."

And indeed, he did put her back up against the hotel room's wall on that late Friday night and she'd enjoyed every single moment of it. And for all of the hotel's lack of multiple stars of acclaim held by the Raphael—where she was *not* staying—the bed was very comfortable for two, though the shower was a little small.

On Friday's flight over she'd identified gaps in her briefing reports, and spent that first afternoon's meeting filling them in, with data from the people who lived and breathed French security.

Sienna had spent Saturday's meetings walking the dicey line of telling someone else how she would run their country if it was hers. If not receptive, at least they'd been very thoughtful by the time the long session was over.

And Saturday night she'd won her bet with herself.

The French President had rejoined them for the wrap-up of the meetings that night and the whole team had sat down to a very formal spread from some of the best chefs in Paris. But it hadn't been half as much fun as that late Friday dinner with the three agents swapping stories around a table so small that their knees kept knocking together. It hadn't even raised a speculative eyebrow from the Parisian agents when she'd moved her chair to sit beside Roy for coffee and dessert as they watched the people of Paris flow by—something she'd never dare try here.

At that ending-night dinner—in tune with her thoughts as ever, or perhaps as concerned with protecting her reputation as her life—Roy had been careful to place himself down the table from her.

And she'd missed him.

It was ridiculous. They'd been within ten feet of each other for days, and she'd missed being able to lean over and drop a line to make him laugh. She'd been able to hear him telling his stories but could only catch enough to know that they were ones she hadn't heard before.

As if to make up for it, Sunday started warm and glorious.

Roy was a generally gentle lover, but he set new standards in the pre-dawn darkness. By the time he was done, she didn't feel sated, she felt worshipped.

She awoke again as dawn was finally breaking. Just like it was supposed to in Paris, the drapes to the microscopic balcony fluttered gently in the breeze as the rose pink light of morning washed across the city and Roy's splendid body.

Sienna watched him for a long while. The July weather was warm enough that he had thrown back even the thin sheet and lay exposed like some Greek statue in repose.

A week and a day.

In a week and a day her life had been altered. Perhaps irrevocably.

Somewhere in yesterday's meetings she had noticed the first shift. She had spent Friday being the investigator and Saturday morning being the coach. But by the afternoon she had indeed been the National Security Advisor for the United States of America. She'd been able to help the French piece together new strategies to address the worst of their problems. Nothing had been solved, but there was a lot of promise for a more secure future.

And what of her own future? NSA for six more months. She'd been approached by several strategy consultants before the President's offer had preempted all others. She knew those offers would be renewed when she left the White House. If she didn't screw it up in the next six months, her future was sound.

Then what?

Children with Roy?

Marriage to a man willing to rage against the ministers of France in her defense?

That had been the true test. Not how he made her body feel. Not his obvious honor and integrity. Oddly it was his fury that had proved his true feelings to her. The depth of it, the complete outrage on her behalf. No agent merely concerned with his protectee's safety would have ranted so. If that was all it had been, he'd have lodged a complaint with their Secret Service and run it through channels.

Roy Beaumont. Always careful. Always steady. He was a forthright man who always spoke his mind. What had it cost him to peel back that layer on his emotions?

She smiled down at him still sleeping beside her.

Did he know that he loved her?

Did *she* know that she loved him? She nearly laughed aloud. Sienna Arnson loved a man. Loved *this* man sprawled naked in the light of a Paris dawn.

She tried to judge the future against this newfound present. Was he a man she could love all her days and he the same of her? "There's a dumb-ass question," she could practically hear Roy say, he'd said it more than once during the meetings. "You can plan for the future, but you can't predict it," his follow-up rarely softened the blow. More than once he'd cut through the chaff and political backloops with his forthright…Yankeeness.

Could she picture starting a life with Roy?

More than any man she'd ever met.

She brushed her fingers ever so lightly along his cheek. He woke as he always did, one instant out, the next totally present. But this time it wasn't the agent who woke beside her, but the man.

Sienna then set about proving to the man just how she felt about that change in who he was with her. When she'd driven him past speech, past control until her merest gesture made him quiver, then she'd straddled him and finally let him send them both to a place she'd never been with any other man.

Chapter 10

It's July 14th," Sienna said as she wandered naked out of the tiny shower.

"Which means what?" Some remote part of Roy asked the question.

The rest of him was too busy admiring the naked woman before him. Not merely her body, which was impossibly firing off some thoughts that they had only just finished exhausting. But also the thoughtless ease with which she moved as she dried and buffed herself with a towel. The wet look was exceptional on her. Her dark red hair had slid into the deepest auburn, its wet tangle emphasizing the strong lines of her face. And her fair skin had reddened to a warm luster from the blazingly hot water she preferred.

But it was the internal contrast that was distracting him the most at the moment. She was soft, welcoming, eager, and sweet. He knew her expressions when enjoying a meal among friends, the look a half instant before she laughed, and at the moment of a cascading release shuddering down her frame.

He also knew her looks when thoughtful, diplomatic, or completely frustrated. The last was revealed by an absolute calm and a solid bastion of silence that was wholly formidable. He'd watched her teasing Mabel Chen and standing up to the Presidents of both the US and France.

The many moods of Sienna Arnson. He could imagine spending a long time learning them, though he doubted he'd ever understand them all. He wondered how she'd look lazing beside a Vermont waterfall after a long fall hike through the oaks. How her face might age with wisdom and joy.

And a part of him desperately wanted to know how soon he could entice her back into bed so that he could again brush his fingers over those amazing curves.

"Roy!"

"What?" She stood facing him, hands on hips, and stark naked except for the towel clenched in one fist. How was a man supposed to think with such a view.

"Speaking here, Beaumont."

"Lusting after your incredible body, Arnson." Which was when he realized Sienna never stood like that herself. She was merely imitating his own stance when she was frustrating him.

She threw the towel at his face then turned for her suitcase.

He admired the view from behind until she was dressed.

When she finished—as if her sleek capris, open sandals, and blouse just thin enough to hint at the black bra beneath wasn't equally distracting—she once again faced him and planted her feet, again mocking his style.

"Listening to me now, Beaumont?"

"Nope!" He made a point of looking her up and down, another image he'd store away for a long time and savor.

"Bastille Day. *La Fête Nationale. Le quatorze juillet.*"

"Is that like Romeo and Juliet?"

"Not in any way, except that this Romeo might soon end up as dead as week-old toast."

"It seems unfair."

"What does?" A light flush of irritation colored her cheeks. Gods but she was fun to tease.

"The peasants overthrew the Bastille prison in 1789 and beheaded poor Louis the Sixteenth and dear Marie let-them-eat-cake Antoinette in '92. And you think that's an excuse to go party?"

She stuck her tongue out at him.

He keyed his radio, "You two awake and ready for breakfast yet? We have a parade to go watch."

Jankowski mumbled something that might have been, "About goddamn time."

"How?" Sienna demanded.

"Downstairs in five," he keyed off and shrugged negligently. "I know shit. It's my job."

"Should I thank Chen or Jankowski for educating your dumb Yankee ass?"

"I'm hurt," Roy slapped a hand to his chest. "You said you liked my ass."

She rolled her eyes and he used her momentary inattention to cross the two steps that separated them and crush her against him. She practically purred as he held her hard.

"How the hell did you become so important to me?"

"It's your job," she mumbled into his chest.

It wasn't funny. It wasn't that he wanted her. It was that he could *not* imagine living without her. Not today, not tomorrow, not in ten years.

For a day and a half he'd sat in meetings and watched her heart. Her commitment to helping. Her gentle hand with ministers and military men who needed a good smack. The only one in the room with a whole clue other than Sienna had been General Dumont. As old as Sienna's father and sharp as hell. He had been the one to clue Roy in on Sunday's importance to France. He had planned to stay until Monday "because even National Security Advisors get the occasional day off," as Sienna had informed him, but this was even better.

The general had told him of the day's events and where to be for the best experience.

And it started with the largest and oldest military parade in all of Europe. Down the Champs Élysées from the Arc de Triomphe to the Place de la Concorde. The President had invited her to stand beside him at the end of the route, along with ambassadors of many countries. It had only taken the slightest glance from Sienna for her security detail to respectfully decline.

"Thank you, Roy," she'd told him as soon as they were alone. "It would be quite an honor, but I'd rather go play. Besides, they'd probably turn it into another meeting and I'm tapped dry."

He let his smile tell her that he had no complaints about her decision. "You gave them a lot. They now need to take ownership of your suggestions or they will remain as solely your skills rather than them making them their own."

"And when did you get so smart?" He remembered the warmth of that moment. Sienna was brilliant and for her not to think him a burden was a gift.

"Sniper, remember?" It was surprising how often that was the answer to her questions. He'd learned about the difference between training and deeply integrated skills with thousands of hours of practice. But he had never realized how ingrained his role had become in his life.

Yet Frank Adams had seen more than just "sniper" in him. No one jumped from counter sniper to head of detail. And now that he thought about it, neither had he. He'd always picked up the scut work of planning and analysis. Only now in retrospect did he understand that Adams had sent that type of work his way far more than he did to others. He'd also been team leader of his sniper squad for the last year which had involved management skills as well as ensuring a deep integration into other teams: ground prep, close protection, SWAT, and air.

"Roy? Where did you go this time?"

"A, uh, far off land filled with naked dancing women."

"Give me a break."

"They're all redheads, and they elect you their queen."

"And I make you the court jester."

"Works for me."

"Any chance of getting a straight answer from you today?"

"Apparently not," but he could see she wasn't as amused as he'd hoped. "I'm finding my world is a little out of its familiar balance since the moment you walked across my scope sight."

"Is that a good thing or a bad?"

He kissed her quickly and shooed her toward the door. "It's neither one. It's the best thing."

And she was, the best thing that had ever happened to him.

#

Sienna liked being someone's "best thing." Even more, she liked being Roy's "best thing."

They bought small strong coffees and large croissants from a tiny shop that fronted the parade route. They applauded the marching troops. Who could resist cheering a cavalry that still rode horses rather than tank-based armored cav or an air cav who flew helicopters. An entire phalanx of marching K-9 unit earned roars of approval from the packed crowds and squeals of delight from the numerous children. A goose-stepping squadron of visiting Mexican falconers in nineteenth-century uniforms complete with hawks and eagles perched on their padded sleeves was a stunning sight. And there was no emotion possible except awe as tanks and mobile missiles rolled down the Champs Élysées.

They climbed the steeples of the Notre Dame cathedral where she snapped a photo of Roy posed with a gargoyle; and Mabel shot a photo of her and Roy with the entire city of Paris laid out behind them.

Roy led them to a quiet lunch in the back garden of the Musée Rodin. It had been the sculptor's home: an open, airy structure filled with magnificent light. If it were a dozen sizes smaller, she could move right in and happily never leave. The ground floor was dominated by a large marble of an intimately kissing couple. *The Kiss* which sounded even more luscious in French, *Le Baiser*. The garden itself was dominated by a greened-over bronze of *The Thinker* and dozens of his other works.

Chen punched him in the ribs for making some crude conjectures on what the three meter high statue was thinking up there atop his stone pedestal. She'd taken to doing that after she determined that their height difference was too great to smack him on the back of the head. It looked as if she threw good punches, not that they fazed Roy in the slightest.

Beneath the shade trees—on a lawn anonymously populated by dozens of other French couples and families on holiday and so green it might have come from an artist's palette—they ate Brie, thin slices of salami, and marinated artichokes on torn-off sections of fresh baguette. Because the three agents were on duty, they all four had soft cider rather than red wine. It was easy to forget she was actually the center of a very safe sphere of protection except when she noticed how rarely they looked at her and how thoroughly they watched the crowds.

She was reminded of Roy in the Smithsonian National Museum of Air and Space. He hadn't spotted her by glancing at the crowd, his gaze had tracked through the hall in a careful sweep until it had alighted on her.

That evening, no one complained about the long wait for a boat cruise along the Seine.

"Teach me to do what you do."

"Guard people?" Jankowski sounded skeptical.

"No, shoot people," Mabel stated.

"Neither," Roy said, of course reading her intent along with her question. He must have noted her watching them watch. "Okay, Sienna. We're standing in a queue of people, what do you see?"

She began listing them, "A bridge, some buildings…" she was able to name more than a half dozen of them, "…the Seine, a queue of people, a departing boat, a—"

"That's enough. Now point to the places you just named in the order you named them."

As she swung her arm back and forth, up and down, she began to feel foolish. She was like a wind-up clock on steroids pointing high, low, back and forth. Roy let her continue until she reached the end of her list—she had to guess at the order of a couple of them—and she could feel the heat in her cheeks.

"Now let's try this. Turn in a slow circle, only looking at what is exactly in front of you as you turn. Try not to look too obvious about what you're doing."

She did a slow casual turn.

"Now what did you see?" He asked when she once again faced him.

It was far easier to list them in order. Also, she would be able to turn back to just the right angle to locate any one of the things she'd seen. Again, he let her run down all that she could recall.

At the very end, while he was busy nodding in a job-well-done fashion, she whispered to herself, "And the man I love." There was no hesitation this time. No second thought. No clench in the stomach.

Her world rocked as if they were already on the boat instead of still standing on the stone quay that had remained unchanged for perhaps a thousand years. In a desperate grab for equilibrium, she shot out a question to buy herself a moment.

"Okay, wise-ass Beaumont. Tell me what *you* see."

He didn't look away from her for even an instant. He also hadn't scanned the crowd when she did. For all she knew he hadn't even glanced around in the last five minutes.

"At one-thirty I see a woman who is either from the central Sahara or is about to collapse from heatstroke. Either way, she's far too warmly dressed for a July day in Paris, so I'm keeping an eye on her. At four o'clock," Roy waved a hand negligently off to his right without turning, "is a man who has been standing at the exact center of the bridge for over ten minutes. He is alone yet doesn't appear to be waiting for someone as he isn't looking around. He is just watching the boats load and unload. A company agent keeping an eye on his investment? A writer busy thinking about his next novel? Or perhaps a shooter watching for a target? Or maybe he just likes boats? At six-thirty, behind me, someone has Chen's attention, so I'm keeping my eye on her to see if her 'person of interest' acts in a suspicious manner."

"Actually," Chen spoke up, "it's just a really cute guy. I don't see squat."

Sienna couldn't tell if she was joking or not and decided she'd be more comfortable if she assumed Chen *was* just ogling a cute guy.

"At nine o'clock, Jankowski—"

"Damn, but French babes slay me," he grinned at her and went back to chatting with Chen, but looking elsewhere as if idly enjoying the day.

"Okay, okay," Sienna held up her hands to stop Roy before he could continue. "You made your point."

"With multiple agents, especially undercover as we are today, we can observe a wide field for potential threats without attracting any attention."

Sienna glanced around and they were indeed being ignored. The attention she'd temporarily attracted as she'd turned her circle pointing at all the sights of Paris like a hick from Reims had drifted away. Not a single person had marked their conversation among the general hubbub of tourists eager for a "French" experience on the Seine. She wondered if French people ever rode these dinner boats and somehow doubted it, except perhaps when escorting foreign guests. Roy and his team had attracted no attention because they didn't act in any way out of the ordinary. Even their tone was lightly conversational, blending easily into the background.

"You missed one," she didn't know if she hoped Roy would pick up on the tease or not.

"You didn't let me finish."

"I'll bet you'd still miss this one. Go ahead, tell me about everyone you're watching. But you're missing one, really obvious person." She wasn't going to give him the hint that it was someone who couldn't stop watching him for even a moment. No man had ever made her feel so safe. She was safe in his arms and under his protection.

He didn't fall for it and look about. Instead he squinted at her and used his brain. She could hear Chen snort and cover a laugh when she got it.

Roy's head quirked in Chen's direction, but he still didn't figure out Sienna's riddle.

Jankowski actually found an excuse to turn a slow and careful circle, but he too missed it. Which had Chen snorting again.

Then it clicked in for Roy and he offered that slow smile of his. His lips curved up until she could imagine how his smile would taste. That was the other real gift he gave her. Against all odds she'd found a man who actually *saw* her. Not just the National Security Advisor, but also the woman who Sienna herself had barely known about before Roy.

"Perhaps I did. Won't happen again," he whispered for her ears alone.

Or tried to.

Chen punched him solidly in the ribs, again, and he grunted at the blow.

Then he leaned down and kissed her.

Was it any wonder that she loved this man.

Chapter 11

R*oy helped Sienna down* the stone steps onto the river boat. Not that she needed the help, she was an incredibly capable woman. But he liked the feeling of taking care of her—a way to pay her even a little of the respect she deserved.

He'd been watching the long boats slide quietly by for several hours, disgorging and reloading their passengers. There were tour boats that probably carried several hundred in closely packed quarters as tour operators called out the sights over too-loud sound systems. The dinner boats were filled instead with comfortable tables, each set for one or two couples. Fine linen tablecloths, cloth napkins, shining silverware—it was fine dining for a hundred. Thirty feet wide, over a hundred long, deep enough for a galley below yet still low enough to slip beneath all of Paris' bridges. When they approached, the dockhand had taken a surprising amount of money to pay for the four tickets, but the *maître d'* escorted them like guests of honor to the very bow. They'd been waiting for a no-show on the dinner reservations—another suggestion from General Dumont. Roy made a mental note to ship the man a couple quarts of Vermont maple syrup in thanks.

Sienna had been following his inspection as he noticed exits, the height of railings if jumping overboard was the best option, and so on. He could see her learning what he did minute-by-minute. He could only imagine how his 101-level lesson in observation was now being integrated into national security methodologies and strategy shifts. Sienna's mind worked like that. It scooped up little facts and used them in strange ways.

He'd had his tirade at the start of the Paris meetings and after that managed to mostly keep his mouth shut. Of course—because Roy's luck was running so consistently terrible lately—it turned out that the US Ambassador to France had been in the room. He'd reported the tirade to his boss in horror, who in turn had told the Director of the Secret Service to tromp one Roy Beaumont. It had then come full circle as a seventeen-word e-mail from Adams.

Hear you kicked their asses. They must have needed it bad. But, Brother, you do like living dangerously.

No judgment. No correction. No signature. But he'd left the e-mail thread all of the way back to the US Ambassador to France for him to read. And because Adams did nothing by accident, the message had been clear, "You're on the front line, it's your call. But next time you may want to think a bit first."

That more than anything else demonstrated what had happened to him this last week. He was now head of a protection detail, a politically sensitive one. It wasn't the first time he'd asked himself why the hell he'd ever come down off the roof.

But if he hadn't, then he wouldn't be the man escorting Sienna Arnson to her dinner table in the very bow of a boat on the Seine.

"Totally worth the price of admission."

"What are you talking about?" She sat as he held her chair for her.

"You."

"What price?"

"The hundred changes you've already caused in my life."

"And the thousand to come, Beaumont," Jankowski dropped down beside him without any ceremony, leaving his "date" Chen to take care of her own chair beside Sienna. "Trust me, voice of experience here. Spend five or ten years with a woman and you won't recognize yourself ever again. Hell, one year."

"Yeah, your socks match now. Why else do you think I introduced you two?"

"You're a Philistine, Chen."

"You were a slob, Jankowski."

"I was," he spoke to Sienna. "But it wasn't my wife who cleaned me up."

Roy exchanged glances with Sienna. She was being amused by the fact that they were taking his and Sienna having a lasting relationship as a given. He slid his foot forward until their ankles brushed. She continued watching their dinner companions, but returned the pressure. Her smile was lit by the soft candlelight. He liked it for several reasons.

First, she looked incredible in the warm glow, maybe he should get some candles for his bedroom. He was fairly sure women liked that sort of thing, though he'd be damned if he was buying any of those stinky, scented ones.

Second, he liked it strategically. The light was low, little shades on the candle lanterns kept the light aimed down at the table. It made for better nighttime viewing of the Paris buildings and monuments along the Seine. It also made one individual versus another indistinguishable more than a few tables away.

"So, if your wife didn't clean you up, who did?" Sienna inquired nicely enough that she might even have been sincere.

"I did. First time I saw her I knew I had to do something if I wanted to catch her."

"What about you, Yankee Boy?" Chen rocked her chair back on two legs. "What are you going to change to win this lady?"

"He already did it," Sienna answered for him.

"I did?"

"You did," she looked at him with those deep eyes of hers. "You came out of your precious sky to walk by my side."

"Don't know as I'd have done it for anyone else." Couldn't imagine how she understood the scale of that change, but she did. His Sienna understood even that.

"I know," she mouthed silently across the table.

As least that's what he thought at first. Then he thought back. There had been an extra syllable on the end.

You.

I know you. It didn't fit. Her mouth shape wasn't right for "know."

Then it clicked and he stared hard at her.

She'd said, *I love you.*

Oh crap! It was one of those moments where if you didn't know what to say, you were totally screwed.

But...he *did* know what to say. Much to his own surprise.

Sienna was watching him carefully, awaiting his response to her throwing her heart out on the table.

He sipped at the glass of ice tea the waiter had barely deigned to serve him when there was perfectly good French wine available.

He did love her, but he couldn't let her have all the fun.

She'd started changing him the moment she walked up the White House path fifteen days ago. Not even knowing her, she'd made him think there was more to life, more to *him* than he'd found so far. By the time they met, he was already smitten. And now—god help him—he knew he'd never find another woman like Sienna. He'd never told a woman he loved her. He was afraid it would somehow come out wrong, or choke him or something.

So he made a different choice.

"About time," he whispered back to her.

Her laugh of delight lit up the evening. And for once Chen was seated too far away to give him one of her "Atta Boy" thwacks.

"Yow!" a sharp pain lanced up from his shin where it had just been kicked.

Chen's grin was appropriately evil.

And for once, Jankowski hadn't missed a thing.

Chapter 12

Sienna had obviously entered some sort of a dream state.

Four weeks ago, she'd been in a Fort Bragg think tank, analyzing the communication architecture of worldwide political information by the US Commands. Then with no explanation as to why, she'd been flown to D.C. and interviewed for three straight days by the outgoing NSA, the White House Chief of Staff, the President, and a laundry list of others. One week spent with the outgoing NSA and she'd landed in the chair.

Now, at the end of her second week as National Security Advisor, she'd consulted with the powers of France and been listened to most attentively. Even without Roy's "icebreaker" they had been open to suggestion; after it they had been truly respectful. By the end they were asking her if she'd like to come work for the French government instead—and she didn't think they were merely being polite.

Best of all—also absolutely the most surprising—she was sailing through Paris with the man she loved. And he loved her back.

They had nibbled on crostini with Brie and slivered fresh basil while opposite Notre-Dame. Eaten an exquisite French onion soup as they floated by the Passerelle des Arts. Dined on steak au poivre as they passed between the Musée du Louvre and the Musée d'Orsay. A strawberry crème brûlée was soon to be served along the packed tables of holiday merrymakers. They were a very happy and content crowd.

The evening was so warm that she'd have been fine, even without the gray-and-gold woven shawl Roy had insisted on buying her. It was beautiful work though, and she wrapped it as tightly around her as a hug.

"Sienna on the Seine. They should make a movie about me."

"You've got the best damn luck I've ever seen, Yankee Boy," Chen shook her head in obvious disgust. "Or perhaps Ms. Arnson does—with the exception of being stuck with yourself."

"Why?"

"We get to watch the Eiffel Tower blow up from a boat on the Seine!" Jankowski practically crowed.

"Damn good show," Chen offered in her Midwest declarative style.

"They're blowing it up?" Roy blinked in surprise and all three of them burst out laughing. Roy took it well, as he did everything except challenges to her safety.

"Fireworks show, Yankee Boy," Chen was the first to recover enough to explain. "Bastille Day, it's the best show of the year and Ms. Arnson lucked into a spot on one the boats that will be floating by the tower for the show."

"Remind me not to make reservations in the future," was Roy's only comment. The wait in line had been a long one—those willing to wait to take the spots of no-show reservations. And he'd done it for her without knowing how huge the payoff was.

"There are days I love this job," Jankowski said, then grimaced. "But the wife will kill me when she hears."

"So, don't tell her. You can trust me to keep your secrets," Chen's tone implied absolutely not.

Sienna looked at Roy. Still he scanned the distance, ever reliable, ever vigilant. What secrets would he keep for her? Anything. And what would he tell her? Anything she asked. He might not think to volunteer something, but he'd answer any question truthfully.

"Roy?"

"Uh-huh." But she knew she didn't have his attention.

"Roy?" She tried it a little louder.

It wasn't until Chen glanced at Roy and then twisted around to see where he was looking, that she felt the first prickle of chill. She pulled her shawl closer and turned as well.

Over her shoulder, the Eiffel Tower soared above the river bank. It was still well ahead of them, but they were crawling slowly toward it along with the clutter of boats jamming the waterway. She glanced at her watch—11:20. The show should start in just a few minutes. Parisians dined late and celebrated even later.

"What is it?" Chen whispered.

"It's called the Eiffel Tower, Mabel."

But she didn't smile or even respond. That's when Sienna identified the look on Roy's face. He was no longer scanning. It was that moment of recognition in the Air and Space Museum, the moment before his eyes had bugged out in surprise.

Target acquisition.

He pulled out the pack that he'd shoved under his chair and dug out a pair of binoculars. They weren't little tourist binoculars; he'd been carrying high-powered sniper binocs with him all through Paris. He always had the backpack, and she'd never given it a second thought.

"Jankowski. Is the Tower opened or closed for a fireworks show?"

"Closed. They clear the people off early for safety during the show."

"The riggers should be long since done."

"Mid-afternoon," Chen confirmed.

Sienna looked at the angle of Roy's inspection, then tried to follow the line up to the Eiffel Tower. At first she thought they were spots in her eyes from staring so hard. Then she remembered what Roy had said about exactly that. "You see more with a relaxed open eye."

She tried relaxing and the spots didn't go away. "Those are moving lights on the—"

"Keep your voice down. Steady and conversational." And in just that tone, he asked, "Which of you is a better spotter?"

"Jank," Chen said. "And don't think that doesn't piss me off."

Roy passed the glasses to Jankowski.

Then Roy rose from his seat, taking his pack with him, and moved around to the narrow space between her and Chen's backs and the ship's bow. The tour company hadn't left a lot of space there, but somehow Roy fit in despite being a big man. It also was an unlit space and made him nearly invisible to the other passengers.

Out of the corner of her eye, she could see Roy pull out something else.

A rifle scope. What else did he have in that bag?

She decided she'd rather not know.

Using only the scope, he began to inspect the tower.

"Damn it," his curse was soft. "I make four, no, five."

"Five," Jankowski confirmed. "Range in the dark? Four hundred meters. First-level restaurant is at fifty meters up. I place them at almost a hundred meters."

"Last minute check of the fireworks?" Chen offered.

"Too last minute," Roy countered.

"Daredevil climbers. Like extreme base jumpers or something. Want the thrill?"

"Nope, next."

Sienna saw what they were doing. Trying to find some rational explanation for five guys up on the Eiffel Tower just minutes before the fireworks show. "Reporters?" she offered. "They're always doing the stupidest things."

"Security at the base is pretty serious," Chen decided. "At least enough to keep stupid tourists and reporters at bay. They had to plan to make it inside."

"Sienna," Roy slipped a laminated card into her hand. It had a list of phone numbers. "Start with Paris SWAT. If they don't respond the way you want, call your buddy Dumont."

Sienna pulled out her phone, "What am I telling them?"

"Two things. Chen, I need all the napkins."

She started collecting them.

"First, don't shoot at the guy in the boat on the Seine."

Chen had collected the four napkins. He folded them in half, laid them together, and wrapped them around something she couldn't quite see. There was the distinct tearing sound of duct tape that had several other table's guests turning. As there was nothing to see, they soon went back to their own conversations.

Then Roy shifted position enough for a lick of candlelight to shine on the barrel of a rifle. He'd taped the napkins around the tip of the barrel. Poor man's silencer. No, a sniper rifle probably already had that. It was a flash suppressor so that he didn't draw any attention.

"Second, tell them they've got at least five suicide bombers up on the Tower."

She heard the soft click as the rifle was assembled and a snap that she was fairly sure was a magazine locking into place.

Sienna had no room for doubt. This was Roy.

She started dialing.

Chapter 13

Roy watched them through the scope.

He needed proof that he was right. He knew he was, but that wasn't enough.

He huddled in the shadow with the rifle resting on the railing as he squatted. But it was useless, the boat was rocking too much.

Order the boat to shore?

They were mid-channel with heavy traffic to both sides. He'd already seen that the dinner boat didn't maneuver quickly. It was designed to mosey along a slow-running river, not deliver troops.

Their actions were wrong for a fireworks team. They were sticking to a single level horizontally rather than moving up or down a vertical line of wiring that might have been tested due to having a last minute problem.

Extreme base jumpers—seeking a showy stunt—would have gone straight to the top.

Reporters would have stayed on the stairs.

These guys were way out on the structure, all lined up along one side.

Demolition work. They were going to cut all of the struts down that one side.

But still, he didn't have proof.

He could hear Sienna getting heated up on the phone and then hanging up with a soft, "*Merde!*"

Even if she reached Paris SWAT, it wouldn't be in time.

"Far left," Jankowski called softly.

He swung the scope. A man stood on the corner strut. He was fumbling inside a pack.

Sienna got through to Dumont and began speaking in rapid French.

The fumbler pulled out a square block of something, and slapped it against the metal.

C4. No firework in the world would have been placed like that. He passed along the sighting and heard Sienna echo it to Dumont.

"Winds aloft?" He couldn't feel crap down in the boat between the river banks.

"I see a flag," Chen replied. "It's not doing much but its moving. Call it ten K from the north-northeast."

"Is that kilometers or knots?" He hissed it out.

"Sorry, kilometers per hour. Told you Jank was better at this. Five knots, give or take."

Roy clicked the scope's adjustment one notch for the effect the light wind would have on his bullet during its long flight. He also rotated the vertical adjustment to compensate for the fact that he was aiming upward at a target, not down. The bullet would have to arc up higher than the target, and then fall to strike home.

"I need something soft," he was on one knee, but he could feel the boat's motion moving him at its whim from his contact with the wooden deck.

Chen handed him a bread roll.

He'd have laughed if he had time. He slipped it under his knee and it squashed flat and useless.

Then, before he had time to ask, Sienna handed him her folded-up shawl. It almost broke his focus. He didn't want this memory attached to his gift to her.

But it was exactly what he needed so he dropped it on the deck without comment.

He loosened his hips the way Kee had taught him until his leg could move separately from his torso. He would hinge at the hip and keep his torso and hands steady.

Roy flipped off the safety.

He sighted, let a small correction from some deep-honed instinct shift the crosshairs slightly left of the target.

Then—for better or worse—he rested his finger on the trigger and began to apply the two-point-seven pounds of pressure he had it set for.

Chapter 14

Sienna would never forget how surreal the event was. She and Chen sat as if casually chatting while they provided a shadow for Roy.

In reality, she was on the phone with Dumont who was working multiple phone lines in the background.

Chen was relaying information from Jankowski as spotter.

Everything conversational. Nothing happening here, folks.

Except Roy was…

She was turned just enough to see the napkins he'd taped in a tube around the barrel flop about. There was no flash, no bang. The shot itself was no louder than the small crackers and other noisemakers that were in use along the shore. More noisemakers on the boat were adding additional cover. Chen was spinning a wooden toy that gave out a sharp "Clack! Clack! Clack!" as she quietly relayed instructions.

"Don't waste time, buddy," Jankowski had said right before Roy shot. "If one of them figures out what's happening, they might throw some manual trigger."

Roy didn't shoot every heartbeat, but perhaps it had been every other.

It was about every twenty of hers—she was surprised her heart could even beat that fast.

"That's five," Jankowski announced. "All look to be clean hits."

"Dumont," Sienna echoed the reports over her phone, "says that a SWAT sniper got two more around the other side."

"Must be strapped in. None of them fell, But I don't see any movement," Jankowski reported.

The first firework went off. It made her jump, but there was no unwarranted explosion along with it.

"We didn't have a chance to warn the firework display controller before that first one," Dumont continued speaking over her cell phone. "But we're having him not set off anything on the level the bombers were working. We have a special squad headed up there right now to clear the bodies and explosives. The fewer people who know about this, the better."

Silently Roy packed away his weapon. There was a smell of scorched cloth from the improvised napkin silencer. But that soon faded.

He settled back in his chair as they were serving the crème brûlée.

"I believe that we'll need fresh napkins," Chen said.

Sienna didn't know whether to laugh or to weep.

All of her discussions with the Parisian authorities. All of their preparations. All of the hatred of a bunch of crazies. And it had ultimately come down to one observant man sitting in the right place with the right hardware—and it had all lasted under five minutes.

In a world of asymmetric warfare, that's what it came down to.

The strategies of her predecessor were going to have to be completely rethought. She'd known of the existence of small, unreported events that were resolved without the public's knowledge. The former NSA had told her how the future First Lady had saved the President's life, unreported. Delta

Force took down drug lords and warlords with near perfect invisibility. Drone strikes were public, but when it was a two-man strike team on the ground, what the drone saw was never reported.

The world had changed irrevocably. Since the American revolutionaries had hidden behind trees rather than marching in the open to face the British, the balance had shifted. The recent wars in Iraq and Afghanistan had brought the lesson home.

And as she'd just seen, the trend was continuing. Rather than giving her a chill, it made her eager to get back to work. There had to be methods to achieve what Roy had just done on a consistent basis.

Fresh napkins were brought.

She missed her shawl. Glancing behind her chair where Roy had knelt, she didn't see it in the shadows.

"Where is it, Roy?" Sienna patted her shoulders.

"In my pack. I'll replace it for you."

"No, you won't."

"But—"

"I know what you're thinking, but you're wrong. It will serve to always remind me how safe you can make me feel."

He actually stood and brought it around the table to drape it about her. His grip was strong on her shoulders and she wasn't sure who was comforting who.

Tomorrow there would be a post-mortem and multiple security meetings before they flew back to D.C. But for now it was just the four of them. It might have been a somber table, but it wasn't. But neither was it a joyous one. Instead it was soft-spoken and they all treated each other very gently.

That night when she and Roy curled up in the same bed, they didn't make love. Instead he simply held her so tightly that she could barely breathe.

He held her a long time before he spoke. It was a lesson for her life, giving Roy the space to find his words.

"No amount of training prepares you."

All of those hours on watch, he'd never had to shoot anyone before.

"They were bad people, Roy, bent on doing unreasonable harm. You probably saved hundreds of lives in addition to a national landmark."

"Probably," he admitted at length.

"Head of detail doesn't mean you aren't still one of the top shooters. It also doesn't mean that you don't have feelings."

She could feel his nod against her hair.

He rubbed his hand along her back for a while.

"Hell of an Independence Day," his voice was thick with chagrin.

She laughed and patted his chest. "I need to start teaching you French."

"Why?"

"Because July 14th is not their Independence Day. On the first anniversary of the storming of the Bastille prison, they held a *Fête de la Fédération* to celebrate the unity of the French people even though it was the middle of the French Revolution."

"Unity, huh?"

"Uh huh," she did her best to imitate one of his grunts.

"How do you feel about unity, Sienna Aphrodite?" It was ridiculous, but she was utterly charmed by his nickname for her. She knew she was up on no pedestal, for Roy truly saw her, but still it tickled her.

"We're lying about as close together as can be." Was he actually talking about their unity? As a couple? If he was, he was going to have to say it himself.

"I think we could manage to get a little closer," he rolled until they were lying nose to nose wrapped in each other's arms and she'd hooked a leg over his hips to hold him close.

"We could, if you think you're going to get lucky tonight."

"Oh, I think I have an inside track on that," Roy tone was far too self-assured even if he was absolutely right.

"What makes you so sure?" Sienna brushed her lips over his.

"Unity Day," he kissed the tip of her nose.

"July fourteenth."

"*Le quatorze juillet.*"

"That's what they call it," Sienna agreed.

"Say you'll marry me, Sienna." His voice turned suddenly harsh and thick with emotion. "Say you'll be my wife through thick and thin, good and bad, because I don't know how I could ever live a day without you."

Sienna couldn't imagine how she'd live a day without Roy.

But his speech—rough and all mixed up in need and the evening's events—wasn't what she wanted between them. There would always be love and truth, this she knew. And safety, because nobody delivered that like Roy Beaumont.

But she also wanted a lightness in their unity. She wanted Sienna Aphrodite as well.

"Marry you?" She did her best to sound a little puzzled by the idea. She hadn't quite forgiven him for saying "About time" when she'd said that she loved him. She leaned back just enough to see the truth in his eyes revealed by the Paris lights which glowed through the soft curtains.

He nodded tightly.

"Sure," she kept it light as if the most important change in her life was of little consequence.

Then she stole one of Chen's lines.

"Yankee Boy."

About the Author

M. L. Buchman has over 40 novels in print. His military romantic suspense books have been named Barnes & Noble and NPR "Top 5 of the Year," nominated for the Reviewer's Choice Award for "Top 10 Romantic Suspense of 2014" by RT Book Reviews, and twice Booklist "Top 10 of the Year" placing two of his titles on their "The 101 Best Romance Novels of the Last 10 Years." In addition to romance, he also writes thrillers, fantasy, and science fiction.

In among his career as a corporate project manager he has: rebuilt and single-handed a fifty-foot sailboat, both flown and jumped out of airplanes, and designed and built two houses, Somewhere along the way he also bicycled solo around the world.

He is now making his living as a full-time writer on the Oregon Coast with his beloved wife. He is constantly amazed at what you can do with a degree in Geophysics. You may keep up with his writing by subscribing to his newsletter at: www.mlbuchman.com.

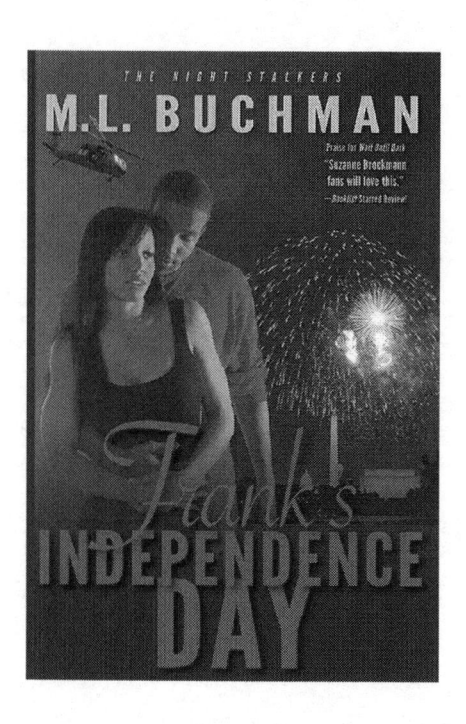

Frank's Independence Day
(excerpt)

Frank: July 4, 1988

Frank Adams had his boys slide up around the metallic-blue late-model BMW at the stop light on Amsterdam Ave. One stood by the passenger door, one ahead, one behind, and he took the driver's window himself as usual.

It was only the third time they'd done this, but Frank saw, without really watching, that they made it look smooth. They'd split the thousand that the chop shop had just paid for the Ford they'd jacked and two grand for the Camry. But a new Beemer?

That was a serious score. What they were doing so far uptown this late on a hot, New York night was the driver's own damn fault.

He started it like any standard windshield scam. Spray the windshield to blind the driver, then shake them down for five bucks to clean it so they can see to drive away. The bright bite of ammonia almost reassuring to New Yorkers who had come to expect the scam. He'd long since learned to flick the windshield wiper up so that the driver couldn't just clean their own damn window. It was when the driver's window rolled down, and the person at the wheel started griping, that the real action would begin.

A glance to the sides showed not much traffic. Lot of folks gone down by the water to watch the fireworks, or off with family for July 4th picnics at the park, or on their fire escapes in the sweltering summer heat. The acrid sting of burnt cordite hung like a haze over the city from a million firecrackers, bottle rockets, M-80s, cherry bombs, and everything else legal or not. Hell, Chinatown would be sounding like they were tossing around sticks of dynamite.

Night had settled on the roads out of Columbia University and into his end of Manhattan, and as much darkness as could ever be happening beneath the New York City lights had done gone and happened.

Frank's boys were doing good. At the front and back, they'd leaned casually on the hood and trunk of the car not facing the prize, but instead watching lookout up and down the length of Amsterdam Ave. They'd shout if any cops surfaced.

And no self-respecting BMW driver would run over someone they didn't know just to get away, especially ones who weren't even looking at them threateningly.

Other drivers were accelerating sharply and running the red light just so they weren't a part of whatever was going down at the corner of Amsterdam and midnight.

Three minutes. That meant they had about three minutes until someone nerved down enough to find a pay phone and call the cops and he and his boys had to be gone.

They'd only need about one.

The Beemer jerked back about two feet with little more than a hiss and a throb from that smooth, cool engine.

His boys were on the pavement before Frank could even blink.

Japs had been sitting on the trunk but was now sprawled on his face and Hale sat abruptly on his butt when the car's hood pulled out from underneath him. It was almost funny, the two of them looked so damn surprised.

Then he was facing the rolled down window, just as he'd planned. He could taste the new-car fine-leather smell as it wafted out.

What he hadn't planned was to be staring right down the barrel of a .357. Abruptly, all he could taste was the metal sting of adrenaline and the stink of his own sweat.

He'd seen enough guns to know that the Smith & Wesson 66 was not some normal bad-ass revolver.

He was facing death right between the eyes.

His body froze so hard he didn't even drop the knife nestled out of sight in his palm.

The woman who looked at him, right hand aiming the gun across her body, left hand still on the wheel, had the blackest eyes he'd ever seen. So dark that no light came back from them, like looking down twin barrels of death even more dangerous than the gun's.

A cop siren sounded in the distance, but his boys were already on the move out of there.

"They're leaving you behind."

Her voice was as smooth as her weapon. Calm, not all nervy like someone surprised by a carjacking or unfamiliar with the weapon she held rock steady.

"What I told 'em to do."

"Don't risk the whole team?"

He shrugged a yes.

That siren was getting louder and it was starting to worry him. But even doing a drop and run, well… He was fast, but not faster than a .357. He stayed put. Classy lady in a Beemer and a dead carjacker, she wasn't risking any real trouble if she gunned him down where he stood.

"Decision point. Go down for it. Spend some time in juvie—"

"I'm twenty, twenty-one next week." Why'd he been dumb enough to say that? Not that the cops wouldn't find out, but they didn't have his prints anywhere in their system… yet. He didn't carry any ID either, but there was only so long you could play that card.

"Okay, do some time or get in the car."

He looked into the deep well of those dark eyes, allowing himself three heartbeats to decide what the hell she was up to. The sharp squeal of cop tires swerving around some other car too few blocks away won the argument.

Frank moved around the front of the car fast, flicking down the wiper blade as he went, and slid into her passenger seat.

While he circled, she'd shifted the big gun into her left hand. Could shoot with either hand, that took training. Some off duty cop in a Beemer, just his luck.

He was barely in the car when the fuzz rounded the corner, their lights going.

"Buckle up."

It was only after he buckled in that another thought struck him. A bad one. She just might drive him somewhere, gun him down, and dump his body. Never knew with cops in this town. Then she wouldn't even have to fill out any damn paperwork. *Little bit late to think of that shit, Adams. Dumbass!* Once around the passenger side, he should have just kept running, not climbed into the lady's damn car like a whatever it was that went to the slaughter. Sheep? Calves? Something. Frank Adamses.

She slid the gun under the flap of her leather vest so that it was out of sight, but still aimed at him across her body. She ran the windshield wiper and together they watched the blue-and-white roll up fast. The cops pulled up driver to driver, facing the wrong way on the street to do so.

"Everything okay, ma'am?"

Frank had the distinct impression that even though the woman was reassuring the cop, if Frank so much as flinched, there'd be a big, bad hole in his chest and that the thing that would really tick her off was the damage to her German-engineered car door where the bullet would punch a good-sized hole after making a real mess of his body on its way through. It took her long enough to talk the cop down that Frank had time to register how the car's seat fit to his body. It was way more comfortable than any chair or sofa he'd ever slouched in. Damn seat alone probably cost more than everything he owned.

Finally satisfied, only after blinding Frank with a big flashlight a couple of times, the cops rolled away real slow. He'd purposely dressed okay in his best jeans and a loose button-down shirt he'd worn to Levon's courtroom wedding. That way he wasn't too scary for the windshield-washing scam to work. It paid off now, he didn't look too out of place in this classy car. He eyed the woman carefully, as classy looking as her vehicle. Or even more.

She pulled her hand out from under her vest of dark leather even finer than the seat upholstery, leaving the gun behind, and rolled up the window. Shoulder holster. He'd tried to carjack a woman who wore a .357 in a shoulder holster. What were the chances of that kind of bad luck? Well, one in three. Third carjacking ever, woman with large gun. Not exactly high-level math.

Though he'd never heard of anything like it on the street. He'd been told to watch for crazies, diving for glove compartments and purses, so full of nerves that they were more danger to themselves than anyone else. Best advice on those had been to run. Toward the back of the car. Make yourself a hard shot when they're all buckled in and facing forward. They'd be undertrained, have lousy aim, and probably wouldn't shoot if they thought they'd won. That's if they could find the damn safety.

Not this lady. Cool and calm.

He'd bet she could execute his ass without havin' a bad night's sleep.

"Let's go somewhere and talk." With the window up, the air-con dropped the temperature about twenty degrees from the July heat blast going on out in the real world which was sweet, but left a chill up his spine that started right where his butt was planted in the fine leather seat.

She punched the gas and popped the clutch, in seconds they were hurtling downtown on Amsterdam and Frank knew he better hang on for dear life.

Available at fine retailers everywhere

Other works by M. L. Buchman:

The Night Stalkers
The Night Is Mine
I Own the Dawn
Daniel's Christmas
Wait Until Dark
Frank's Independence Day
Peter's Christmas
Take Over at Midnight
Light Up the Night
Christmas at Steel Beach
Bring On the Dusk
Target of the Heart
Target Lock on Love
Christmas at Peleliu Cove
Zachary's Christmas
By Break of Day
Roy's Indepedence Day

Firehawks
Pure Heat
Wildfire at Dawn
Full Blaze
Wildfire at Larch Creek
Wildfire on the Skagit
Hot Point
Flash of Fire

Delta Force
Target Engaged
Heart Strike

Thrillers
Swap Out!
One Chef!
Two Chef!

Deities Anonymous
Cookbook from Hell: Reheated
Saviors 101

Angelo's Hearth
Where Dreams are Born
Where Dreams Reside
Maria's Christmas Table
Where Dreams Unfold
Where Dreams Are Written

Eagle Cove
Return to Eagle Cove
Recipe for Eagle Cove
Longing for Eagle Cove
Keepsake for Eagle Cove

SF/F Titles
Nara
Monk's Maze

Sign up for the newsletter to receive news and free items:
www.mlbuchman.com

Made in the USA
Middletown, DE
22 December 2016